Full Circle

A Bindarra Creek Short and Sweet Romance

and

A Clever Christmas

A Bindarra Creek Christmas Romance

Annie Seaton

Dedication

To Ian, my partner in life and love.

Full Circle

A Bindarra Creek Short and Sweet Romance

Annie Seaton

Chapter One

Sydney, Friday 12th April

Cleo Ainslie closed the old book with her usual care, her fingers lovingly caressing the soft leather cover, but her mind was elsewhere. As soon as she'd seen Paternoster Row, London, as the place of imprint in the 1798 tome, her thoughts had left the workroom on the bottom floor of the State Library of New South Wales, and rare books were suddenly the last thing on her mind.

It happened every time she saw the imprint, Jonathon Kendall and Co. behind the title page, and she always opened the London published books of this particular era slowly, willing her thoughts to stay focused on the restoration task ahead of her, scared that she'd see that name and be reminded of her heartbreak. Even if it wasn't a Jonathon Kendall imprint, her thoughts would swoop off in that direction and invariably her day would be ruined. But she'd learned to overcome the sad thoughts, and regrets—Cleo enjoyed her work in the Special Collections department of the library, and if she occasionally was confronted by a name that brought sad memories to the fore, so be it.

As far as she knew it was a coincidence, *her* Jonathon—oh no, forget that, he hadn't been *her* Jonathon for a long five years—had no connection with the eighteenth-century printing house. Jonathon Kendall of twenty-first century Australia was a cattleman in the north west of New South Wales, fifty kilometres outside of Bindarra Creek, the small country town where Cleo had grown up.

And where she had found and lost her first love.

Her only love. She shook her head with a sigh as she placed the book on the side of her desk and pulled off her cotton gloves before glancing at the old-fashioned clock on the wall near the door. It was a solitary occupation, and although she enjoyed her work restoring rare books, she didn't *love* it. One day she would follow her dream and start her own business.

Soon.

Enough of the reminiscing and daydreaming, she told herself sternly; she had half an hour to tidy herself up and get to the restaurant at Circular Quay before she was due to meet her friend, Richard Treloar.

Five minutes later, Cleo had walked out of the library onto Macquarie Street and looked around with pleasure. The last of summer was hanging on with a relentless grip, although the last few mornings had held a slight chill when she'd walked around the harbour at sunrise. Sitting at a desk all day necessitated a morning and evening walk, and Cleo had seen a lot of Sydney since she'd started work at the State Library since graduating from university two years ago.

The early evening sky was a deep blue, darkening as the sun moved closer to the horizon, with shards of golden cloud picking up the fading light. The traffic was heavy as the Friday afternoon commuters made their way home for a weekend of freedom. In the distance she could smell the salt tang of the harbour and hear the squawking of the seagulls that were constantly on the search for food scraps.

As she stood waiting for the pedestrian light to change to green at the corner of Bridge Street her phone trilled in her pocket. She glanced down, surprised to see it was Richard. For a brief moment, she hoped he was cancelling and then guilt trickled through her and she injected a bright note into her voice.

'Hi, Richard. I'm just walking down to the harbour, now.'

'Hello, Cleopatra.' As always, his words were precise and formal, and Cleo frowned. Ever since they'd started seeing each other—friends only and *not* with benefits, she'd told Chrissie on many occasions— and Richard had discovered that her legal name was Cleopatra, he'd insisted on calling her by her full name.

She held the phone close to her ear as the light changed to green and she set out across the street.

'Don't rush, my dear,' he said. 'I was late getting out of court, and I have to meet with the judge. A difficult case today, with an unexpected outcome.'

Cleo read between the lines. He must have lost his case, and if there was one thing Richard hated, it was losing. Cleo grimaced; the last thing she felt like listening to over dinner, was the ins and outs of an industrial case that he had said was impossible to lose.

He obviously had, and it would be in the forefront of his mind.

Again, the guilt flowed in. Richard had been very kind to her, since they'd met at a library function last year—his mother was a library patron—and she enjoyed his company.

Most of the time.

'I'm fine if you need to cancel,' she said brightly.

Hopefully.

'Oh, no. I have something very special planned tonight, and then we're going across to see

Mother after we have dinner. I've changed the reservation from six to seven thirty, so you've got time to go home now and put something lovely on.'

Cleo looked down at her navy skirt and pale blue blouse. In consideration of Richard's penchant for fancy restaurants, she'd added a muted paisley scarf to her outfit, and a pair of small gold earrings. The last thing she was going to do was catch the ferry across the harbour to her apartment at Mosman to "put something lovely on."

'I'm fine. I'll see you at seven- thirty.' Before he could argue—and he was very good at that—she disconnected the call and slipped the phone back into her handbag. Slowing her pace as she walked down the hill, Cleo considered her options. She had time to go back and work for another hour, but the thought didn't appeal. Ever since she'd seen Jonathon Kendall on the imprint, her thoughts had been in Bindarra Creek. With a brisk nod, she stepped out again; she'd go down to the harbour, sit on the grass in the park under the bridge and call Gran. That would get it out of her system; a few minutes of gossip about Bindarra Creek, what Mrs Lette and Mrs Miller had been up to, would help Cleo settle back into her cosmopolitan lifestyle in the big smoke as Gran always called it.

One thing that Gran knew not to discuss was

Jonathon. The first time she had mentioned him when Cleo had left for Sydney, Cleo had made it quite clear that Jon was a no-go topic of conversation. Her friends from Bindarra Creek, Chrissie and Janice, who had moved to Sydney the year before she had, knew that as well. For all she knew Jonathon could have flown to the moon; she didn't know where he was, what he was doing, who he was with now and nor did she care.

I don't.

So why do you spend so much time thinking about him, the little voice of her heart said. It's been five years girl, get over him.

Yes. I will.

Cleo walked past the ferry terminal at Circular Quay and walked along the pavement in front of the Museum of Contemporary Art. The foreshore was busy with tourists and the Friday night crowd heading for the bars for an end-of-week drink, and by the time Cleo reached the bridge, she decided to go back and sit on one of the benches outside the museum. It was getting a bit too dark to go anywhere away from the crowd.

As she pulled out her phone to call Gran, it buzzed in her hand and she answered the call.

'Cleo. It's Chrissie. Have you left work yet?'

'I have. I'm down at the harbour. Dinner

with Richard has been put back a bit and I was just about to ring Gran for a chin wag.'

'She's not there.'

'Where is she?' Cleo frowned; she really should ring home more often.

'She and Auntie Bette have gone on some sort of book cruise thing with a group of librarians.'

'What, from Sydney?' Cleo looked over at the cruise ship—Pacific Dawn— that was docked across the bay. 'Which boat?

'No, out of Brisbane. They left yesterday, a ten-day cruise listening to some guy talking about his book. But listen, enough about that. Jan and I have just knocked off and we need to see you. We'll meet you at Jacksons at a table outside. See you in ten.'

Chrissie disconnected before Cleo could reply, but she didn't mind. She had been friends with Chrissie and Janice since kindergarten at Bindarra Creek Primary School, and even though they didn't see each other as much as Cleo would have liked—they were all busy with their respective careers—it was good to know they were around if she needed someone.

With a lighter step than before, she walked the short distance to the popular bar in George Street.

Chapter Two

'Over here.' Chrissie's shrill whistle turned heads of the dark-suited executives enjoying a Friday night drink.

'You can take the girl out of the country, but you can't take the country outta the girl, hey?' Cleo crossed to the table.

'No, you'd be right at home in the paddock instead of the flash boutique you manage now.' Cleo hugged Janice and Chrissie before she slipped into the spare seat beside Chrissie. Chrissie was dressed to the nines in a royal blue silk dress and Cleo looked down at Chrissie's shoes. She had to lean forward to make herself heard over the voices and the traffic going past.

'I don't know how you walk in those heels.' Cleo shook her head.

'I have to look and sound the part, daaarling.' Chrissie grinned as she put on the posh accent she used all day.

'So what's so urgent you needed to see me immediately?' Cleo picked up the rum and Coke that was waiting on the table for her. For a moment, she considered checking she had some breath mints in her bag, but then shrugged. Richard didn't like her drinking anything other than the top-class Australian wines that he thought he was an expert on, but stuff it. It had been a long week, and a rum and Coke would go down well.

Chrissie and Jan exchanged a look before Janice leaned forward.

'Did you get your invitation?' Jan said. 'I thought you might have called, but it's getting close now and you haven't mentioned it.'

Cleo frowned again. 'Invitation to what?

'The reunion,' Chrissie butted in.

Cleo shook her head. 'No. Reunion of what?'

Again, that shared look between her friends. Suspicion niggled for the first time.

'Bindarra Creek High. At the Bowling Club.'

'No, I didn't, and I wouldn't go anyway.' She picked up her drink and narrowed her eyes as Chrissie leaned forward and put a beautifully manicured hand on Cleo's wrist. 'As you well know.' Cleo's tone was firm.

She hadn't been back to Bindarra Creek since she'd left the day after Australia Day five years ago. Her excuse had been that three years of university, and then two years of work kept her too busy to do the eight-hour drive, but Chrissie and Janice knew the truth.

And Gran.

Some of it, anyway.

Gran made sure she came to Sydney to see her at least twice a year. And in her Christmas holidays, Cleo always flew up to north Queensland to visit her parents where they'd bought a sugar cane farm, just south of Townsville. So, there was no reason to go home.

None at all.

And a school reunion wasn't going to entice her back there either.

And it wasn't home. *Sydney* was home.

Chrissie raised her eyebrows. 'We're both going, Cleo. And I've booked three adjoining rooms at the Fig Tree Inn. It will be great fun. A chance for the three of us to have a weekend away together.'

'I hope one of those rooms isn't for me?' Cleo held her friend's gaze. 'No way. Not a chance in hell. It's not going to happen.'

Janice Presland was the quietest of the three and her soft voice was almost pleading as she put her hand on Cleo's arm beside Chrissie's. Jan and Cleo had sat next to each together that first year of school, and their bond was unbreakable.

'Come on, Cleo. Isn't it time you put the

past behind you? Things have changed, and it won't be the same without you. We'll have a ball.'

Cleo frowned, and she knew the scowl on her face was dark. The ever-present guilt tugged again as disappointment marred Jan's pretty face.

'Not my idea of fun, I'm afraid. What could possibly be fun revisiting the past, in a town I couldn't wait to get out of?' She moved her arm away from the gentle grip of her two best friends. 'Now be honest, you two were the same. Why would you want to go back now?'

'How long since you've been home?' Chrissie sipped her cocktail and regarded Cleo intently.

'It's not home. This is home now.' Cleo gestured to the busy city around them.

'Home is where the heart is.' Chrissie winked at Janice and Cleo burred up, knowing how she could wind her friend up.

'Richard is where my heart is,' she said demurely, but there was a hint of steel beneath her words that Chrissie should have recognised.

'But he's a jerk—'

Cleo shook her head. 'Don't start, Chris. Okay?'

'Come on, Cleo. I'm just teasing. Besides Jonathon won't even be there.'

A shaft of familiar pain replaced the guilt

that had previously been sitting in her chest.

'I think he's overseas at an export convention,' Janice added quietly.

'Well, you two are really up-to-date about the goings on in good old Bindarra, aren't you?' Cleo looked at her empty glass with surprise. 'I'm getting another drink, do you both want another one?'

By the time she came back from the bar with the three dinks, she had composed herself.

'I'm sorry I snapped. I hadn't heard about the reunion and it came as a surprise. I guess they don't have my current address. Who's organising it?'

'Nina Potter,' Jan replied.

'Oh.' Cleo ignored the heavy feeling in her chest and took a deep swig of her rum and Coke. 'And just so you know Jonathon Kendall has nothing to do with the reason I'm not going, even if I wanted to. I've used up all my holidays and flex days, so I don't have time to travel up there and back. I wouldn't care if he was there or not. That's past history now. *Ancient* history.'

This time the look exchanged between the other two was triumphant.

'But you can,' Chrissie said. 'It's on next weekend, Easter Saturday, and you've already told me that Richard is going sailing with his lawyer mates.'

'Four days to get there and get home. Come on, Cleo. Please? It won't be the same if you're not there.'

'The three musketeers, remember?' Chrissie said with a laugh. 'Us against the cool group. I can't wait to tell them about my boutique in the Pitt Street Mall. We can all get dolled up and wow them.'

'In something "lovely",' Cleo said under her breath.

'What?'

'Nothing,' she said with a small smile.

'And the Fig Tree Lodge,' Jan said. "Remember how we used to walk past it when we sneaked off from school to get hot chips at the Cypress Café when we were in Year 12? We imagined staying there when we were grown up and rich.'

Cleo laughed. 'We used to wag Mr Chalkley's geography class more than we went to it.'

'I guess we weren't so good after all,' Chrissie said with a giggle. 'We booked it because it's close to the bowlo. We can have a few drinks and walk back.'

'It's probably nowhere near as good as we remember. Although it was a bit old and decrepit inside I remember Gran saying.'

'Mum said that Mrs Lette's had it all done up. Apparently, it's the place to stay,' Jan said.

Nostalgia flooded though Cleo and she was tempted to say yes. Before she could speak, her phone buzzed, and she put a hand over her mouth when she saw the time.

'Woops.' She grabbed for a mint from her bag as she put the phone to her ear. 'Sorry, Richard. I'm just in a cab now. I'll be there in five.'

Chrissie jumped to her feet and whistled again, and a vacant taxi cruised to a stop at the kerb near the table.

'Love you pair.' Cleo put her phone away and reached over and hugged Janice, and then Chrissie. 'I'll think about it. But don't get your hopes up. Okay? I was going to spend Easter setting up my website.'

As Cleo climbed into the taxi, she narrowed her eyes as her two best friends high-fived each other.
##

Richard was standing impatiently at the door of the restaurant at the Quay as Cleo paid the taxi driver. Her thoughts had been in turmoil on the quick drive down, and she took a deep breath, trying to find the serenity that Richard preferred. As he took her elbow to escort her into the restaurant, he bent down to her upturned face and dropped a light kiss on her lips.

'Pretty scarf, darling. But a dress would have been better.'

Darling? That was a first, and it made Cleo feel uncomfortable. As had the kiss.

As they were shown to their table, Richard's light banter was out of character. She was surprised. When he lost a case, she usually had to jolly him out of a bad mood.

'So, tell me about your day. What wonderful old books did you acquire today. Anything interesting?'

'Yes, a beautiful old book on birds with a fore-edge painting from a London publishing house in the late eighteenth century. It took me most of the day to work with it.'

'Wonderful. Would you miss the job if you weren't there?'

'Bits of it. But as you know I have a plan. Why do you ask?'

This time his tone was dismissive. 'I've already told you that sort of online business wouldn't be successful.'

Cleo's quick temper was well known to her friends, and they knew how to recognise the signs. She reached up and carefully tucked her hair behind her ears and lifted her chin, but Richard had already moved on. She bit down the angry response that had bubbled to her lips.

'I'm sorry I was late, but it couldn't be helped. Anyway' —he gestured to the waiter — 'we're just going to have an entrée here and then Mother is cooking a celebration dinner for us.'

Cleo's eyes widened as the waiter placed a silver ice bucket on the table and placed two crystal glasses in front of them. 'You won your case?'

'No.' His face darkened for a moment. 'But we're not going to worry about that.' Richard reached into his pocket and drew out a small silver case. 'I have better news.'

Cleo's eyes widened and her stomach churned as her gaze stayed on the case.

Surely not?

'I've been offered a position with one of the top Melbourne firms and I've accepted. I know this is premature, but I think it would work out well. Now that I'm in such a prestigious position, I'll need a wife to help me set up a successful life down there. Cleo' —Richard took her hand and flipped open the case — 'I would be greatly honoured if you would become my wife.'

Cleo pulled her hand back, searching for the right words. Richard had been good company for her over the past year, but theirs certainly hadn't been a romantic relationship. Her voice held confusion. 'But Richard, we don't love each other.'

'Perhaps not, but I think very highly of you, Cleo. And you will be eminently suitable. Mother agrees. I can give you a very good life.'

Maybe it was the two rums that Cleo had had that prompted the laugh that broke from her lips. 'Eminently suitable?'

He nodded gravely, still not picking up on her mood.

'Richard, I'm sorry. If you think that, you don't know me at all. There is no way that I would marry without love.' Her laughter had gone, and her tone was sad. 'I've known love once, and I won't settle for second best.'

'I wasn't aware that you were seeing someone else.' His voice was stilted, and he snapped the case shut and put it into his pocket, his mouth set in a straight line.

'I haven't been although I had a perfect right to if I'd wanted to. It was a long time ago, and I was badly hurt. I thought I knew what it was like to be loved unconditionally, but I was wrong.'

'So, all the more reason to listen to me. We could—'

'No, thank you.' Cleo lifted her hand up. 'It's been fun spending time with you, and I wish you well in your new position. Say goodbye to your mother for me. I hope her dinner isn't spoiled by my refusal.' Cleo stood and picked up her bag. She pushed past the waiter and left Richard sitting there, his mouth open and a red tinge on his elegant cheekbones.

Chapter Three

Good Friday - Bindarra Creek

Jonathon Kendall closed the gate of the house paddock and stood watching the sky as the sun slipped below the horizon. He shivered, not so much from the autumn chill, but at the sight that filled his vision. Dry, cracked paddocks, empty of stock. He'd sent the last of his stock to market after the muster last week and wasn't going to restock his five hundred acres until the rains came.

If they ever came. He was going to help his father out over on the main property and maybe pick up some contract work in town.

If he could. Maybe he'd have to go further afield.

Work was scarce; many of the local farmers had already walked off farms that had once been lush and productive; farms that were now dry and barren, and the men and women were now looking for work in the small country towns that dotted the north west of New South Wales. Russ, his older brother had left town before the drought took hold. Not only had he abandoned the family, but disappointingly he'd left his responsibilities behind too.

Two years ago, Jonathon had made enough money from his cattle sales to buy new equipment and move to the cropping that he'd always planned. Chick peas had been a certainty in the export market and when the dry first began further north, prices had gone up, and Jonathon had planned to capitalise on the demand. He'd kept a few cattle while he researched his crop. There'd been no point in going to the exporters' conference that he'd planned to attend, and there was no spare cash to justify it.

No one had predicted the drought that had taken such an awful hold over the past two years.

He looked up at the cloudless sky; a sky that hadn't delivered a drop of rain for five hundred and twenty-one days. His plan for cropping had been put on hold; he didn't know how long he could last out here.

With a frown, he ignored the sound of children's laughter coming from the house; he wasn't in the mood for playing with the kids this afternoon, like he usually did.

Jonathon turned and walked to the shed, dust with the consistency of talcum powder kicking up from beneath his work boots. He was expected in town and was supposed to be staying at the Fig Tree Inn for the weekend. The complimentary accommodation had arrived in the envelope with his printed invitation to the school reunion. He felt a bit guilty about going; he'd only gone to Bindarra Creek High School for his senior high school years, and besides, the thought of accepting charity didn't sit comfortably with him.

The memory of those years after school still had the power to upset him, but he could put that away now. He had enough worry with the drought, and how he was going to manage. Maybe he could hand the acreage back to Dad. Jonathon shook his head; he couldn't do that, he had commitments now.

A deep sigh welled up as he took another deep breath. He opened the door of the ute and glanced at the back seat. His packed bag was in there; he'd call in and let Dad know that he was going to town for the weekend. Dad would keep an eye on Cathy and the kids.

Maybe he'd go the reunion.

Maybe he wouldn't.

With a roar, the ute revved and this time the dust hung high in the air as Jonathon drove down the three kilometres to the front gate.

***

The drive from Sydney did Cleo a power of good. Richard's attitude and the invitation to the reunion had been the catalyst she needed to push her out of the half-world she'd been living in for the past five years. Her sudden departure from Bindarra, and her refusal to return had been cowardly, and the reunion was a perfect time to put that behind her. Chrissie and Jan had been delighted when she'd called and said she'd go with them. Things had almost gone awry when plans had changed at the last moment. Chrissie had to work in the boutique on the Saturday morning.

'There's no way I'm missing out,' she'd said when she called Cleo on the night before they were due to leave. 'I'm going to fly up and hire a car at Armidale. Jan drove up today; she wanted to see her mum on the way, but she'll be at Fig Tree Inn in the room adjoining yours by the time you get there. I'll arrive in plenty of time for the dinner, so I'll see you there. We're at a table with the old gang.'

'The old gang?' Cleo asked carefully, and Chrissie had waved a dismissive hand.

'Chelsea, Gary, Bobby…no one else.'

Cleo had briefly reconsidered, and then decided she would still go. 'Okay. I'm sort of looking forward to it. Sort of.'

'It'll be great fun. Listen, I've got all the details for our rooms. Apparently, there's a newfangled system. It's all paid for and there's no one there to check the guests in. There's a key pad on the front door and then a different one for each of the rooms. Hang on a minute.' There was a rustle of papers and then Chrissie continued. 'You're in room six on the top floor. I'll email you the code.'

'Thanks. Safe travels. I'll see you there.'

The gum trees flashed by as Cleo approached Bindarra Creek late on Good Friday. The further northwest she'd travelled through the day, the more the dry paddocks and emaciated cattle had surprised her. She'd known there was a drought, and Gran had told her it was the worst in living memory, but seeing it firsthand was a shock. The land was dying, and it broke Cleo's heart. The lush green paddocks of her childhood were brown and withered. Maybe it was an idealised memory; how could she have stayed away so long? If she was honest, this was where she belonged. Maybe not in Bindarra Creek any more—that would be too hard—but out here in the country. Away from traffic, and smog, and the crowds of people that were Sydney.

No one, not even Chrissie and Janice—and most certainly not Gran—knew the level of hurt that Jonathon Kendall had inflicted on Cleo the year she'd turned twenty.

Their future had been mapped out and she had been so happy. Working part-time at the Bindarra Creek Library had topped off a perfect life as she and Jon had planned a future together. When they'd got engaged, just after Cleo had turned nineteen, his father had sectioned off five hundred acres of the cattle property and put it under Jonathon's management, and Cleo had spent many weekends out there, helping him. They had drawn up plans for the house and dreamed of a future together. Her parents had moved north to their new farm in the tropics, and Cleo was living at Gran's.

'Six bedrooms,' Jon had said one night as they stood looking at the house site on the top of the hill. One for us and one for each of the kids we'll have.'

'Only five?' Cleo had giggled and bumped his shoulder. 'I want at least ten.'

The wedding plans were well under way, and the house plans were with the council.

'We'll be back a month before the wedding, sweetheart,' Mum had said as they'd left to head to their new life in the north. Dad had wanted a change and had bought a sugar cane farm at Giru, up near where Mum had grown up. 'It's time we moved away for a while. Your grandparents are getting on, and I want to spend some time with them.'

'I'll miss you Mum, but Jon and I will come visit,' Cleo had said with a smile. 'He's taking me to Hayman Island for our honeymoon.'

'That's beautiful.' But her mother had frowned before she'd gathered Cleo in close for one last hug. 'I worry about you marrying so young.

You know we love Jon, but are you sure it's the right decision for you? No university? No following your dream?'

'I can study externally, and yes, Mum, I am sure. I'm following my dream. I've already started planning my online book business.' Her reassurance to her mother was now like the dry dust that blew along the road as she travelled west.

Her dreams had been destroyed just as Hayman Island had been destroyed in that devastating cyclone a few years later.

Jon and Cleo; the dream couple at the end of year formal. The couple everyone sighed over.

Their relationship had been sweet; she'd known from the minute he'd walked into the science laboratory in Year 10, that Jonathon Kendall was the one for her.

And he had been, until that horrendous day five years ago when Nina Potter had come to the library to see her just before closing one afternoon. Cleo had listened to what Nina had to say, and left the library unattended, walking out in a disbelieving daze. She'd run down the path, around the corner, past the pool and the tennis courts to witness the truth for herself.

Her Jon had been head-to-head with Cathy Keppel in the Royal Hotel. Cleo hadn't even gone in, but she'd seen them through the large arch that led into the main bar.

Cathy's arms were around his neck, and Jon hadn't pushed her away. He'd lowered his head to touch hers and hadn't looked up. The bar was full of the late afternoon drinkers, and he didn't seem bothered by the fact that the world could see him. The world of Bindarra Creek.

I was young, and naïve and trusting.

Within a week, Cleo had moved out of her room at Gran's and headed for Sydney. She wasn't going to give Jon the satisfaction of being the one to break off their relationship, and she'd thought long and hard about the words she wanted to use before she wrote to him.

Dear Jonathon,

I've done a lot of thinking recently, and I've decided to leave Bindarra Creek. I've realised I'm not the one for you, and you're not the one for me. The thought of settling down as a farmer's wife makes me feel constricted. I want to see the world, I want to go to university. I know you need someone who can help you, and you'd hate the thought of a wife who felt tied down.

Please don't try to see me or change my mind. I've decided and that's the way it's going to be. It would just be painful to talk this out. I'm sure you'll meet someone who will be happy to share your life.

I wish you well.

She'd written it in longhand on notepaper and hoped that he had shared it with his new girlfriend.

Cathy Keppel. The new girlfriend who according to Chrissie's best friend, Nina, was already carrying Jonathon's child.

Chapter Four

When she stopped at Tamworth for fuel, Cleo scrubbed at her cheeks, cross with herself that the memories had brought tears to her eyes. This journey was one of renewal, and healing; the first step in her new life. As much as she enjoyed her position at the State Library, it was not what she wanted to do for the rest of her working life. She had a lot of thinking to be done; and plans to make.

She was going to follow her dream and do what she'd always wanted to, even if Richard had laughed at the idea. Back when she'd first thought of the online library service for rural readers, Jon had agreed that there was a place for it. Gran had smiled and said, 'it's a ripper of an idea.'

But there was no place for the past, and no place for tears. Cleo filled up the car at the service centre at the south side of Tamworth, grabbed a hamburger and drove slowly through the small city, looking for a motel to spend the night. Chrissie had booked their rooms at the inn for the Friday night before her plans had changed, and she hadn't been able to change the booking. It was Easter, and there was a one month no-cancellation rule at most establishments.

Of course, it was Easter, and that was why every motel Cleo passed as she drove through Tamworth had the "no vacancy" sign illuminated, so she decided to keep going. It didn't matter what time she got to her accommodation at Bindarra Creek as she was already checked in and had the code that Chrissie had emailed saved in her phone. It was still a fair drive from Tamworth to Bindarra Creek, so she took a long break on the other side of town and bought another coffee to keep her awake. It would be around midnight when she arrived. Cleo knew that the wildlife would be out and about after dark; with the dry paddocks and the bush running out of food, starving kangaroos and other wildlife would venture closer to the roads in search of fresh grass. She'd seen dozens of dead animals along the road as she'd driven through the upper reaches of the Hunter valley, and it had gotten worse the further she'd travelled.

She drove slowly with the lights on high beam and managed to slow down the couple of times she spotted a kangaroo on the road ahead. Her little car would crumple if she hit anything, and she kept her eyes low as well. She remembered the time Dad had hit a wombat; they were like hitting a hunk of concrete.

Finally, in the distance the lights of Bindarra Creek lit up the night sky ahead. The road in was very familiar; the turn off to the east where Jon's family farm was situated on the western foothills of the Great Diving Range was not far out of town. She'd driven that road a thousand times. Cleo straightened her shoulders and stared straight ahead as she drove past the turn off.

There was no going back.

Half an hour later, she pulled up outside the Fig Tree Inn. It was dark, and the front of the house was obscured by the large Moreton Bay Figs that fronted the footpath; there was just a small glimpse of white wrought iron lace edging the top veranda where a light was on at the southern end of the house. The trees had been there for as long as she could remember but Cleo was surprised to see how much they'd grown despite the dry, but when she thought about it, she realised it was seven years since she'd walked past them in her school days.

She had never been inside the historic house, but she knew the stories about the ghost and the history of the building. Excitement prickled through her. Now she was in Bindarra Creek one part of her was filled with a pleasant anticipation, and one with the cold fingers of apprehension. If she could get through this reunion, it would be a step in her growth. She would be able to put Bindarra Creek and Jonathon Kendall behind her.

Maybe, the true path to healing would be to see him again one day. Chrissie said he was overseas at some conference now, so he must be doing okay. Her main worry was that Cathy would be at the reunion. Seeing the woman he'd married— she assumed that they'd married, because Jonathon always did the right thing— would be hard to deal with, but she'd be strong and deal with it. People dealt with the aftermath of failed romances every day; after all, hers was simply a teenage romance. She blocked her mind to the preliminary preparations that had taken place for her wedding.

The drive from Sydney had given her plenty of time to think and prepare for her return to Bindarra Creek. Now that she was here, it was nowhere near as bad as she'd imagined, and she pushed away those last few tendrils of apprehension.

Cleo climbed out of the car, retrieved her bag from the backseat and locked the small sedan. The town was still … and silent. No traffic and no animal noises. The house loomed ahead, menacing and dark as she walked quickly along the path. When she stepped onto the bottom step, it gave out a ghostly creak beneath her foot and Cleo jumped, putting one hand to her chest as her heart thundered. The story of the ghost of Fig Tree Inn searching for her brother flitted into her mind, and she swallowed and reached for her phone to use the Flashlight app as she approached the main door.

Just as Chrissie had described there was a keypad beside it.

Very flash technology for Bindarra Creek.

But nothing would have surprised Cleo; Edwina Lette had always been out there with her waist-length grey hair and baggy clothes, running her psychic service out of the hairdressing salon for as long as Cleo could remember. Holding up the phone she pressed the numbers she'd memorised in the car, and the door opened with a soft click. A dim security light came on in the hall and she stood and looked around for the steps. The timber-floored hall ran across the centre of the house and the stairs leading upstairs were halfway along on the right. A hallstand held a bunch of sweet-smelling roses, and beeswax polish blended with it to provide a welcoming fragrance.

Cleo approached the steps quietly, aware that there were probably other guests asleep in the rooms. As she walked along to the staircase, she peered into the other rooms that were dimly lit. A library was first on the left, and the sight of the floor to ceiling bookshelves filled with books piqued her interest. If she had trouble sleeping, she'd come back down and browse quietly. A dozen or so steps led up to a landing before the stairs turned at a right angle. Across from the base of the stairs was a doorway that led into a dining room. A small fire burned in the grate of a modernised brick fireplace, and the flames reflected on the high gloss of a large dining room table. Her interest grew; this was a beautiful restoration. Last she'd heard the verandas had rotten floorboards and the plumbing and electricity was antiquated.

She stepped quietly onto the staircase but there was no answering creak this time. At the top of the steps the hall went left and right, and Cleo shone the light at the number on the door closest. She was in luck; it was number six. Putting her suitcase down, she keyed in the code and the door opened.

The room was spacious with a pink wrought iron four poster bed on the opposite wall between two lace-curtained windows. She stepped to the open door at the end of the room and smiled when she saw the large claw-footed bath. After unpacking her small case, she took her toiletries bag and placed it on the marble topped washstand on the opposite wall.

An electric jug and a tray with two cups and teabags sat at the end of the marble top. Cleo filled the kettle, walked back into the bedroom and checked the time on her phone. She's made good time considering she'd taken it slowly, and it was just after midnight. Knowing Janice, she was probably still reading in the room next door.

Cleo tapped on the adjoining door, and there was a rustling sound from next door. She pushed the door open. 'I'm here. Are you awake? Would you like a cuppa? We've got something to celebrate.'

On the drive up she'd made the decision to leave the library and focus on her business. Richard's proposal had been the impetus for her decision. She'd saved enough to give it a trial for a year.

The light next to the bed on the other side of the room came on as she walked in.

'Jug's on, I—' Cleo bit back her gasp as a tousled blond head appeared from beneath the pink floral-patterned doona. Familiar green eyes stared at her and the look on the face in which they sat was as shocked as the feelings coursing through her. Her mouth dried, and her knees shook as embarrassment consumed her. She put her hands to her burning cheeks and turned around and fled before Jonathon Kendall could say a word.

Slamming the door between the two rooms, she leaned against it, eyes squeezed shut and face burning.

What the hell was Jonathon Kendall doing in the bed that Janice was supposed to be in? All she could be thankful for was that Cathy hadn't woken up and poked her head above the covers, and seen Cleo making an utter fool of herself.

Chapter Five

When he'd hit town, Jon had gone to the bowling club for the Friday night smorgasbord. It had changed since he was last there, and the Chinese food had been disappointing. He'd had a couple of quick beers before coming to the inn and having an early night. Crashing into bed by ten, he'd gone straight to sleep, exhausted by the worry of the farm, and what he was going to do. He and Dad didn't talk about it much; he'd seen his father's shoulders stoop lower each month. If he could get an appointment tomorrow, he was going to go and see the doc while he was in town, because he wanted to get some advice on mental health. Dad wasn't in a good place at the moment, and the drought was getting worse each week.

Now Jon sat up in bed rubbing his eyes. Had he dreamed that Cleo Ainslie had just asked him if wanted a cup of tea?

Maybe I'm losing the plot too.

Jon looked at the door; a thin strip of light was shining beneath it from the other room. He climbed out of bed and pulled on his jeans and padded across the room, his bare feet making no sound on the timber floor. Standing beside the door, he listened, still wondering if he had been dreaming. If so, the girl of his dreams was identical to Cleo. Gorgeous dark curls framing a beautiful face; dark-brown eyes that had been wide with shock, and luscious red lips that begged to be kissed.

He frowned; he hadn't been dreaming; Cleo Ainslie had come through the door and had been standing by his bed when he'd surfaced from the depths of sleep. Her eyes had been full of shock; the same shock that was now vying with his disbelief. It had been five years since she'd dumped him. The year that everything had gone to shit.

Jon had never got over Cleo. He'd loved her so much; her departure had left a tremendous hole in his life and he'd filled it with work. It had been easy; Russ had left for the first time the same week and there had been so much to do on the farm back then. Bitterness sat in his stomach, keeping company with the sour taste of the worst Chinese food he'd ever eaten.

Anger followed the bitterness, and he crossed to the door and rapped his knuckles on the timber. 'Cleo? Are you there?'

Even saying her name hurt. He hadn't spoken her name to anyone for years; the couple of times Cathy had mentioned her, he'd shut down the conversation.

Silence. God, how stupid would he look if it was someone else in there. Maybe he had dreamed it? He'd bloody dreamed about Cleo most nights for the first two years she'd gone, but he'd been too damn proud to chase after her.

Cleo Ainslie had made her choice and he wasn't a part of the world she'd wanted. Her letter was imprinted on his brain.

'Get over it, son,' his father had advised with the best of intentions. 'You were both too young to know what you wanted.'

All Jon knew was that he'd wanted a life with Cleo.

'Cleo?' This time he softened his voice a little.

The muffled response was indecipherable.

'Can I open the door?'' He tried the handle, but it was locked now. 'Please?'

'Why?' came through the door.

Why? Jon had to think about that. Why did he want to see the girl who'd broken his heart? Even if she had come bursting into his room in the middle of the night.

'I guess I'd like to talk to you. There's a lot of questions I'd like to ask you.'

Are you happy, Cleo? How did your life turn out when you left? Are you married? Do you have children? Why are you in Bindarra Creek? The questions rippled through his mind, but he stood quietly waiting for her answer.

The brass knob turned slowly and then the door opened a crack. 'Do you want to come in here? It's more private.'

Jon frowned. 'Private?'

'I'm in here by myself.' The whisper was quiet.

By herself? What was he supposed to take from that?

With a shrug, Jon pushed the door open and stepped through into the other room. A small lamp on the table in the corner was the only light on in the large room. As Cleo's eyes widened, he saw the tinge of red in her cheeks in the dim light. He looked down at his bare chest and the unbuttoned jeans that he'd pulled on in a hurry, and then looked up, his glance lingering on her. If anything, she was more beautiful than when he'd last seen her. A slim pair of black leggings clung to shapely legs, and a snug T-shirt caressed her pert breasts. Cleo was thinner than she had been in her teens, but it suited her.

He leaned back on the door and crossed his arms; he didn't give a damn if she felt uncomfortable with his appraisal. 'Long time, no see, Cleo. You're looking good.'

She stepped away from him and stood in the

shadowed corner of the room. She nodded but didn't reply.

Jon rubbed his hand over his stubbled chin. He was past due for a haircut, and hadn't shaved this morning so he probably looked like a hobo. He narrowed his eyes as he realised that *she* had come into his room, seemingly knowing that he would be in there. 'What are you playing at?'

She drew herself up straight, and her gaze was glacial. 'What am *I* playing at?'

He nodded. 'You're the one who came in asking me if I wanted to celebrate with you. What are we celebrating? Our reunion? You should have warned me before you booked the room, Cleo. I could have come prepared.'

'Prepared for what?' she asked.

'For whatever you had in mind. When a woman invites a man into her bedroom to celebrate at midnight, what else is he to think?'

'How dare you! I wasn't inviting you. I thought Janice was in there.'

His eyebrows rose, and her blush deepened. 'And I was inviting her for a cup of tea. So get your mind away from where it obviously is.'

'I could cope with you being gay. That would explain a lot.'

'I'm not gay. And explain? What have I got to explain to you?'

Jon kept a lid on his temper. As much as he was enjoying pushing Cleo's buttons, he could see she was upset. 'How about we continue this discussion over breakfast? I'm not at my best right now.'

'And you probably don't want Cathy to know you're in here either.'

'Cathy?' He stared at her.

'Yes, Cathy. Your wife.'

Jon swallowed. What the heck was she on about? And then the penny dropped. Cleo must have heard that Cathy and her kids were living out at the farm and jumped to a conclusion. Until he knew what was going on, he'd play along.

'Ah, my wife, that's right. Don't worry. Cathy's—'

'You haven't changed at all, have you, Jonathon?' Her voice was low and harsh as she interrupted him, and he stared at her as she continued. 'Just go. I don't want to be in your company.'

With a lazy shrug, and the most nonchalant expression he could summon, Jon pushed away from the door. Before he opened it, he turned to her. 'I guess I'll see you at the bowling club tomorrow night?'

Raised eyebrows were the only reply.

Chapter Six

The door closed with a soft click and Cleo fought for calm. Despite her deep ragged breathing she crossed to the door—on tiptoes—and placed her ear against the timber. The bed in the next room creaked and she held her breath and strained to hear voices, but all was quiet. She shouldn't have cut him off when Jon was going to talk about Cathy.

But truth be known, Cleo knew she couldn't have coped.

She turned away from the door and flopped onto the bed, grimacing as it made a huge creak. The bed was lumpy beneath her rigid muscles, and the pillow was hard. Obviously, the renovation had only been for the building so far. She rolled over onto her back and flung a hand over her eyes.

What a bloody disaster! Why on earth had she come back to Bindarra Creek? And what the hell was Jon Kendall doing in the adjoining room. Cleo sat up as the penny dropped. Jumping off the bed, she picked up her phone and pressed the speed dial to Chrissie's number.

It picked up on the second ring, but the voice was groggy. 'Hello?'

'Chrissie Peterson, you are responsible for this, aren't you?'

A lengthy silence, then. 'For what? Is that you, Cleo?'

'It sure as hell tootin' is, and you'll be lucky if I ever forgive you for this.'

'I take it you've arrived safely and you're at the Fig Tree Inn?'

'I am.' Cleo crossed to the window and stared out at the veranda. There was a swinging chair positioned at the end but she sure wasn't going to get to use it. 'I'm packing up now and I'm going to stay at Gran's.'

'You can't.' Chrissie's voice was firm.

'And why can't I?'

'Because your gran has the painters in. There's scaffolding outside and drop sheets all through the house. And the furniture is probably all moved.' A note of desperation had edged into her friend's tone.

'You've thought of everything, haven't you? You set this up, Chris. I know you. You can't leave good enough alone.' Cleo paced the room and focused on keeping her voice low. 'Where's Jan?'

'She's staying at her cousin's house. We could only get the two rooms.'

'So, what about you? I guess you're not staying here either?' Before Chrissie could reply,

Cleo hurried on. 'Well, you can have this room because I'm out of here.'

'There's nowhere to go. The motel out on Mt Ingalls Road is full, and there's no accommodation left at any of the pubs. Everyone's come back to town for the reunion.'

'I thought you said Jon was overseas.'

'He was supposed to be.' Chrissie sounded contrite. 'Cleo, listen to me. And listen to me carefully. Things aren't what you think they are, but it's up to Jon to tell you that. He's never got over you, sweets. Janice and I are just trying to help. We want you to be happy.'

'Happy?' Cleo closed her eyes and took a deep breath. 'Have you got any idea what it does to me to know that the man I loved once is through the door in bed with the woman he replaced me with?'

'Calm down. Cathy is *not* in that room.'

'Are you sure? How can you be sure?' A measure of relief trickled through her.

'Trust me. I know. Follow your heart, Listen to Aunty Chrissie. You know Jan and I wouldn't do anything to hurt you.'

'I know, but I'm not happy.'

'But I'm hoping that by the end of tomorrow night, you will be deliriously happy. You need to be honest with Jon, and he needs to be honest with you. You broke his heart, Cleo.'

'I—'

'Look, all I'm going to tell you is, there was mischief done and you need to trust me. Jan and I only found out when Nina called us about the reunion. Promise me you'll stay there until I get there. Promise?'

Confusion was whirling through Cleo, and a tiny sliver of hope. Chrissie was right; she and Jan wouldn't do anything to hurt her. 'Maybe.'

'Cleo?'

'All right, I won't leave, but I'm not going to the reunion tomorrow night.'

'God you're hard to get on with. I'll see you tomorrow about three, and I've got a dress for you. This one is a stunner.' Chrissie paused for a minute. 'And love? Sleep well.'

Cleo disconnected the call.

Sleep well?

Pah, and pigs might fly.

Chapter Seven

Jon was out of the shower, dressed, and considering his options as someone knocked on the door. He hadn't had a wink of sleep and was thinking about heading back to the farm. Seeing Cleo, albeit briefly in the middle of the night had thrown him for a sixer and he'd lain there awake for a long time before the sun had finally filtered through the lace curtains. He'd thought about going out to the veranda to get some fresh air; the smell of the old carpet and timber was doing his head in, along with the image of Cleo that he couldn't lose—but he didn't want to bump into her out there.

He crossed to the door slowly. Who knew he was in here?

He pulled the door open and frowned as a smiling face greeted him.

'Janice?'

'Yes, that's me. How are you, Jon?' Her voice was a low whisper and she glanced nervously at the door up the hall.

'I'm fine, thank you. What can I do for you?'

'Um, Chrissie Peterson rang me from

Sydney. You and I need to talk.'

Jon scratched his head and stared at her. He felt like he was in a parallel universe or something. Cleo, next door, Janice—he'd forgotten her last name—and Chrissie Peterson on the phone. The three of them had been friends at school, and his suspicion flooded through him. 'Did you have anything to do with booking this room for me?'

She nodded.

Jon pulled his wallet out of his back pocket and his voice was short. 'How much was it? I don't need charity.'

Janice waved her hand. 'Look we'll sort that out later. But right now, I need you to come with me.'

'Where to?'

'To the bakery. We're going to have breakfast—your shout if it makes you less grumpy. We need to talk. Before tonight, before the reunion dinner.'

***

Despite the events of the night and the strange mood she was in, Cleo slept like a log. The long drive and the emotions of the past twenty-four hours had worn her out. A proposal, a midnight run-in with her old love, and the decision to leave her job had led to some crazy dreams. Jon had been in the house that they'd planned to build, but as well as being filled to the rafters with dozens of children, every wall had been filled with rare books. Luckily Cathy hadn't ventured into her dream.

A soft cool breeze playing on Cleo's face woke her. She lay there for a moment; the sun was high, and the faint sounds of cattle mooing drifted in through the window. The inn wasn't far from the paddocks near the showground. The natural sounds soothed her; it was nice not to wake up to the sound of heavy traffic on Neutral Bay Road like she had done for the past couple of years since she'd bought her apartment. Real estate prices had skyrocketed recently, and she'd make a tidy profit on it when she sold it.

And she was going to do that very soon. She'd put her notice in at the library after Easter, and list the apartment, and then all she had to decide was where she was going to settle to start her online business. With internet available throughout the country now, the world, as they said, was her oyster. She could even move up to North Queensland if she wanted.

Quiet voices drifted in from the hall and Cleo frowned. It sounded like Janice. But according to Chrissie, Jan was over the other side of town staying with her cousin. She strained to hear, but the voices stopped. Two doors closed and then all was quiet again.

Cleo lay there for a while, deciding what she was going to do. She'd pretty much promised Chrissie that she'd stay in town, so she'd keep her word. But as soon as she found out what her friends were up to, she was out of here. Her stomach grumbled, and she climbed out of bed.

She was going to have to go out in search of food, but until she knew what was going on or spoke to Janice, she was going to keep a low profile in town.

It was too small a town for her to go unnoticed. There was a truck stop out near the high school on the Tamworth Road; she could go out there and grab some breakfast. There'd be less chance of running into someone she knew.

As Cleo stood under the shower, common sense kicked in. She had no reason to hide or keep a low profile; she wasn't the one who'd done anything wrong. From memory, if the town was still the same she had the choice of the Cypress Café or the bakery for a coffee and a toastie.

It was cooler this morning, so after she was dressed, she pulled the light cardigan from her suitcase before she picked up her purse. She headed for the door, and then hesitated before going back into the bathroom. Picking up her lipstick, she ran it across her lips and then put on a touch of mascara and blusher. Brushing her hair again, she ran her fingers through it and fluffed up the curls. Just because it was a small town where she probably wouldn't see anyone who remembered her, she could still look her best.

Closing the door behind her, Cleo threw a quick glance at the door along the hall, but all was quiet. The rooms downstairs were deserted, but voices came from the back of the house where the kitchen was, and the smell of brewing coffee tickled her nose.

Chapter Eight

The town had barely changed since she'd left. As Cleo strolled along the street and turned the corner towards the café, the only difference was the brown grass crackling beneath her boots and the sad wilting plants. When she'd been at school, the gardens at the front of the houses across from the Fig Tree had been bright and colourful. At this time of the year, the early winter roses should have been colourful and spilling over the weathered picket fences, but there were no flowers and the rose bushes that she passed were straggly.

The bell tinkled as she pushed open the door of the café. The tables were deserted and there was no one in the shop, but the coffee machine was on, and the smell of brewing coffee filled the shop.

As she waited, the half-door to the kitchen swung open, and a woman emerged wiping her hands on her apron. As she looked at Cleo, her eyes widened, and her mouth dropped open. 'Cleo!'

Cleo's heart hammered as her memory took her back to the day that this woman—then a teenager—had delivered the news that had changed her life.

'Hello, Nina. You still live in Bindarra then?'

Nina nodded. 'Yes. I do.' Her chin lifted, and her voice held the same animosity that she'd directed at Cleo since primary school days. 'What are *you* doing in town?'

'I'm here for the reunion.'

'But—you can't be. You weren't invited.'

Cleo raised her eyebrows. 'To my knowledge, it's a reunion for the 2011 year 12 of Bindarra Creek High?'

Nina's head jerked in another nod. 'Yes.'

'Well, I was in that year, so I'm here. I'm curious to know why you thought I wasn't invited though.'

'Because I sent out the invitations. I'm on the organising committee.' Even though Nina's voice was sullen, her chest puffed out with self-importance.

'And I was excluded? Interesting.'

'We didn't know your address,' Nina mumbled.

'Not hard to get from my grandmother.' Cleo smiled a brittle smile. When she was at school, the nastiness of Nina's group—including Cathy Keppel—had given her some hard times, until she'd learned to be resilient, so there was no way at twenty-five she was going to be bullied. 'Anyway,

I'm here now, so I'll see you tonight. Lovely to chat, Nina.' She lifted her hand in a cute wave and headed for the door.

'Um, you don't want to buy anything?'

Cleo turned and shook her head. 'No. I hear the coffee is much better at the bakery.' The parting shot was cheap, but she couldn't help it, and it made her feel better. 'See you tonight. I'm so looking forward to seeing everyone.' Leaving the café, she strode along the footpath and headed for the bakery on Main Street. All she needed now was for Cathy Keppel to be working there and her day would be complete.

But the fates had other plans for her.

It was worse.

Much worse.

***

Jonathon was still trying to come to terms with what Janice had told him when the door opened, and the subject of their conversation walked in. Cleo glanced across at them, and a deep blush suffused her cheeks. To her credit, she kept walking towards the counter. As she stood there waiting to be served, Janice reached over and squeezed his hand.

'It's all up to the two of you now.' She stood and walked over to join Cleo at the counter. She put her hand on Cleo's shoulder and leaned down and spoke to her. As she did, Cleo threw a nervous glance in his direction, and a surge of love filled Jonathon's chest. He shook his head.

Maybe it was going to be all right?

A lot of time had passed since he and Cleo had been together. Maybe too much? Maybe she didn't care enough anymore?

As he watched, Janice took Cleo's hand and led her over to the table. She pulled out the chair she had vacated, and Cleo sat in it, reluctance showing in every line of her body. Her lips were set, and her eyes were cool.

'Stay there, and I'll get you a coffee,' Janice said. She looked over at Jonathon. 'It might not be the best venue to sort this mess out, but it's best that it's done now while you're both here.' Janice went back to the counter, and Cleo didn't speak a word while they waited. He couldn't take his eyes from the beautiful face that he had known so well, the little snub nose and that cute tiny mole at the edge of her cheek.

He jumped when Janice reached over and put a mug of coffee in front of Cleo.

'I'll wait outside,' she said.

Jonathon lifted his gaze and caught Cleo staring at him. Hope shot through him, because he saw the longing in her eyes before the shutters came down and she looked at the coffee in front of her.

He couldn't help himself. He reached over and took her fingers in his and held them tightly. 'Oh, Cleo. Where do we start?'

Her gaze was anguished, and he wanted to take her into his arms and kiss the worry from her face.

'I don't know why I'm here. I don't know why I let the girls talk me into coming to Bindarra Creek, and I don't know why we're sitting here together. I just want to go home.'

'I hope we can, sweetheart.' He kept his voice soft, so he didn't spook her. She was skittish, just like that young mare that he'd been breaking at the farm. He ran his thumb lightly over the translucent skin of her wrist.

'I'll start at the beginning. Mischief was done. Lies were told that made you think badly of me.' He tried to keep the emotion from his voice as he tried to tell her what had happened.

Cleo shook her head. 'It wasn't a lie, Jon. I saw you and Cathy in the Royal that afternoon. The same day I wrote you the letter and left town.' Her voice trembled. 'I don't know why I'm telling you this now because it's too late, but when I saw you there—holding her—something in me died. Nina told me why.'

'Sweetheart. Nina lied to you. Janice told me how jealous she was of you. Nina took an opportunity to cause trouble, and she did. We've wasted five years.'

Cleo stared at him. 'What lies? I heard that Cathy was living out at the farm with you.' Her voice trembled again but she lifted her chin. 'And that you have two children now.'

Jon reached over and held her other hand in his. He needed to show her that he loved her. How much he loved Cleo Ainslie and how he'd never stopped loving her.

'That day you saw us in the pub, I was on my way to pick you up from the library. I had a surprise for you. The plans for the house had been approved. Cathy waved me down and asked to speak to me. Yes, she was pregnant, but to *Russ*, my brother.'

Cleo lifted her head and her brown eyes filled with tears. 'But why . . . how is she living with you now? And there is another child?' Her hands shook in his. 'And you're not married to her?'

'Listen to me, sweetheart. Josie and Billy both belong to Russ. He came back for a while after Josie was born, but he couldn't handle it. He's been gone for two years now. Dad and I took Cathy in; her family threw her out when she was pregnant with Josie. It was never a secret. Everyone knows that the kids belong to Russ.'

'Really? You're not with Cathy? You never have been?'

'No, but I have a gorgeous nephew and niece, and Cathy keeps house for Dad. I've never been with anyone else. I found it too hard to forget about a brown-eyed girl who stole my heart in Year 10. I just can't understand how you didn't find out the truth.' Jon held her gaze and shook her head. 'Please tell me that that letter you wrote me was your way of coping. Tell me you didn't mean it.'

Tears were rolling down Cleo's cheeks, and he lifted one hand to wipe them away.

'Of course, I didn't mean it. It was the only way I could cope. I didn't ever tell anyone that I thought the kids were yours, otherwise Gran and Chrissie and Jan would have set me straight quick smart. Any time they tried to talk about you, I wouldn't let them.'

'Can we start again? Is it too late to take up where we left off?'

Cleo's hand shook as she reached up to tuck her hair back behind her ear. 'It's going to take some getting used to. I'm going to need some time, I think.'

Disappointment raced through him; Jon would do anything that she wanted.

Cleo's eyes were alight as she stared at him. 'At least until tonight.'

Jon stood and pulled her to her feet, before he wrapped his arms around her, around the woman he loved. 'I think I can wait until then.' Her lips parted as she stared up at him, love and certainty shining from her eyes. The past five years were gone as his mouth met hers.

Neither of them heard the whistles from the two bakers in the kitchen, nor did they see the satisfied smile on Janice's face as she peered around the door.

Chapter Nine

Easter Saturday
Bindarra Creek Bowling Club

The Bindarra Creek Bowling Club ladies had outdone themselves in the decoration of the function room for the high school reunion. Despite the drought they had managed to gather enough greenery and flowers from the gardens around town to provide a backdrop of colour. The tables were covered with white cloths left over from a recent wedding, and the plastic picnic chairs were each festooned with a large satin bow. A small crowd of early arrivals hovered around the bar, and the conversation focused on the lack of rain and cattle prices. Gradually the arrivals increased until there was a queue for drinks.

Nina Potter tottered across the dance floor carrying a tray of name tags; her stiletto heels clicking on the parquet floor. She parked herself at the end of the bar and proceeded to call out names, loudly chastising anyone who declined to wear their name tag.

'Give it a break, Nina. You're not in school

now,' Bobby Dawson called out. 'We all know who everyone is.' He turned his head as Gary Clarke tapped him on the shoulder.

'Maybe not, bro.'

Bobby shook his head as a tall, well-dressed woman with fair hair walked in. 'Don't be stupid, you know that's Chelsea Morgan. She taught your kids.'

'Not her. Look at what—I mean who— just walked in behind Chelsea. I'm in lurve.' He put his fingers to his mouth and let out a piercing wolf whistle. Heads turned as three women walked through the door and paused at the side of the room.

'Hubba hubba.' Bobby ogled.

'Way out of your class, mate.' Jon Kendall stood beside his classmates and smiled as the three women crossed to the bar.

'Bloody hell, that's Chrissy Peterson, and Janice Presland and—' Bobby cut short as Jon's hand descended on his shoulder.

'And Cleo Ainslie, my fiancée,' he said proudly.

***

Dinner had been served and cleared, and the dancing was well underway. Cleo sat back in her chair relishing the warmth of Jon's touch. He hadn't let go of her all day; the only time he'd let her leave his side was to get ready for the reunion. They'd walked along the river and talked all afternoon, catching up on the years they'd missed.

They'd reached the weeping willows where the river headed south, just past the caravan park. Jon had stepped her behind the curtain of graceful foliage and his mouth had explored her lips, her cheek and her neck until Cleo was short of breath.

'About tonight?' she asked shyly when he finally lifted his head.

'Tonight?' Jon repeated as his hands caressed her shoulders.

'Your room or mine?' Cleo looked up at him from beneath her lashes. She still had to pinch herself to believe this was real.

He smiled down at her. 'I don't care which one as long as you're in it.' His voice took on a serious note as he pulled her closer. 'But we've only got until Monday and then you have to go back to Sydney, I guess?'

She nodded. 'But not for long. I was moving anyway.'

'Where to?' Jon asked, a frown wrinkling his tanned face.

Cleo shrugged but she knew her eyes were sparkling. 'I'm open to suggestions. It can be anywhere. I'm finally starting up my online library service.'

'That's fabulous. I'm so pleased you

realised your dream. You've had that for a long time, sweetheart.' He regarded her intently. 'So you could do it from anywhere?'

She nodded.

'I know a hill where a beautiful house was going to be built. The plans have been approved but—'

'But?' she asked.

Jon shook his head. 'But times have been tough with the drought and we might have to reduce the number of bedrooms. Our ten kids will have to share.' His smile was wide, and Cleo couldn't resist standing on tiptoes and putting her lips against his.

'They won't, you know,' she murmured against his mouth. 'I have an apartment in Sydney that's going on the market that will probably add a second storey and another five bedrooms.'

'We've come full circle, haven't we?' Jon had said.

Full circle. They had.

'Come on you pair, time to hit the dance floor.' Chrissie's voice interrupted Cleo's thoughts as she sashayed past firmly in Bobby Dawson's grip.

Jon pushed his chair back and stood holding out his hand. 'May I have this dance, Cleo?'

She lifted her hand to take his, and the engagement ring she'd carried with her for five years sparkled in the fluorescent light.

'I'm so pleased you didn't send that back to me,' Jon said as he led her to the dance floor.

'I tried to about eight times, but I couldn't bring myself to do it.'

'Just as well, because I probably would have ditched it in a temper if it had come back to me. But we're all good now, aren't we?'

Cleo nodded. 'There's only one problem that I can see,' she said.

Jon frowned as they stepped into a waltz. 'Problem?'

'When can we set a wedding date? I'm not going to risk losing you again. If I come back to town, Nina's still here.' But her words were softened by a teasing smile.

'Leave Nina to me. When's your gran back from her cruise?'

'Next week.'

'And how long until your parents could get here?'

'Um, about a week I'd say when they hear the news.' Cleo shivered as Jon's lips found that sweet spot below her ear.

'Okay then. Is three weeks enough to organise a wedding? We've wasted enough time.'

'Three weeks is fine by me. Just let me check with my bridesmaids.'

Cleo waved to Chrissie and Janice and called them over. Bobby Dawson and Gary Clarke weren't far behind them.

'Hey, you two meddling witches. I have something important to ask you.'

The satisfied smiles on Chrissie's and Janice's faces were enough of an answer.

'Three weeks it is, Mr Kendall.' Cleo looked around the room and a flood of happiness filled her. 'I'll be home in two, married in three and this time I'm home to stay.'

THE END

A Clever Christmas

A Bindarra Creek Christmas Romance

Annie Seaton

Dedication

To Ian, my partner in life and love.

Chapter 1

Leah Maclean waited while Joe Rossiter parked his work ute over near a tractor shed about fifty metres from the old homestead. The December afternoon sunshine was hot on her bare arms, and she walked across to wait in the shade of a bushy orange tree. The last of the blooms had drifted to the ground after the light shower of rain last night and the faint fragrance of orange blossoms hung in the air.

'Bit hot for you out in the bush, hey, Leah?' Joe's grin was wide as he sauntered over to join her in the shade of the tree, a couple of kelpies sniffing at his legs.

'I'm used to the air conditioning in the city, but this is wonderful.' Leah gestured around her. 'The gorgeous clear sky and the clean air—no traffic noise or smells! The green of the bush and the birdsong tells me I'm finally home.'

'So, it's good to be back in Bindarra Creek? It's still home to you?' Joe held the gate open for her and they walked along a circular drive edged with colourful summer annuals. 'How long are you going to stay? Just the holidays?'

Leah hesitated before answering. Not

because she was being secretive, but because she was still uncertain where her future lay.

She shook her head and sighed, her shoulders slumping. 'I haven't decided yet. I'm a shocker at decision-making. Even though it's ten years since I moved away to uni, I felt at home again as soon as I drove into Bindarra Creek the day before yesterday. I knew I would. I've got lots of great memories from growing up here. I had good friends, and we had such fun times in our high school years.'

'Really?' Joe frowned. 'I didn't think there'd be that much here for teenagers.'

'We made our own fun back then. We were a tight group.' Leah was thoughtful as she walked beside Joe. He was a good-looking guy: tall with broad shoulders, a ready smile and great manners, and she imagined he'd be popular with the local girls. It was good to have made a new friend in town so quickly; they'd met at the pub the night before last when Leah had walked to the Riverside Hotel for a bistro meal. Maybe spending some time with Joe would help her forget about Mark. Purely platonic of course. Her problem was, there was absolutely no spark when she looked at Joe Rossiter—just the pleasure of talking to a nice guy.

'How did you make your fun in those days?' he asked.

'Picnics and swimming in the Akuna River in the summer. Hiking and camping in the national park in the winter. I guess most of my friends were like me. We loved being outdoors.'

'Any still live here?'

'I don't know. I lost touch with everyone because I haven't been back for such a long time.' Leah shook her head as Joe opened the gate for her, and blocked the dogs from following them into the house yard. 'Maybe some do. We scattered far and wide after school, but my closest friends went into careers that were motivated by our love of the landscape here. My best friends, Ruth and Natalie, headed off to different unis to do environmental science, and our mate, Jack, went to Armidale to study agriculture.'

'What about you? What did you do in Sydney?' Joe asked. They'd only shared brief backgrounds when they'd met at the pub. It had been very kind of Joe to invite her out to the Christmas barbeque today. Good old country hospitality.

'I did my studies in natural illustration. I've been working at the Botanical Museum in Sydney for the past six years.'

'Sounds interesting.'

'Yes, but time for a change, I think. If I move back here, I'm going to start illustrating children's books. I have a couple of freelance jobs already. But I have to see if I can make a living out of it.'

'I enjoy living and working in Bindarra Creek, but not for the long haul. I'll move away eventually. Buy my own place somewhere, but that's a long time in the future.' Joe said. 'You never know some of your old friends might be here this afternoon. I think Jac and Ryan are having quite a big do.'

'That'd be great, but I doubt if any will be around. Last I heard Jack was running an irrigation project in the west, and Nat and Ruth are both overseas,' Leah said with a smile.

'Half the district will be here. We came early so I could help Ryan with the cooking. He might be a good builder, but my brother is not an expert when it comes to barbecuing. So even though your friends have moved away, you're thinking of leaving the city and coming back to Bindarra Creek?' Joe shook his head. 'It would be a quiet life.'

'I think it would suit me, but I have to give it some more thought before I decide.'

'How long are you staying at Fig Tree Lodge?' Joe asked.

'Until the New Year, and then there are a few holiday bookings arriving,' Leah replied. 'I have to decide what I'm doing and see if I can find somewhere to live if I do decide to stay. 'It's strange not having my family here, even after all these years. Mum and Dad moved to Brisbane while I was at uni, and my sister is a nurse up in Cairns. I might even head up that way if it doesn't work out here.'

'If you do decide to stay, rental accommodation is tight, but I know that Grant—you'll meet him this afternoon—has a duplex that will come up for rent soon. I'm going to move into one of them, but I'm pretty sure he hasn't let the other one yet. I'd be a good neighbour. No wild parties.'

'Could be a plan,' Leah said.

'Keep it in mind.' The look that Joe gave her held something she wasn't quite sure of. 'Come on. I'll introduce you to everybody,' he said as they reached the house.

Leah linked her arm through his. 'Sounds good. Lead me to the festivities, kind sir.'

Her thoughts were jumbled as the sound of voices came from the back garden. If it hadn't been for Mark Altmann, she probably wouldn't have left Sydney or her job, but she knew that being back in the bush would be a distraction from her unrequited love.

A ripple of worry trickled through Leah as

she wondered if quitting her job on the spur of the moment *had* maybe been a bit hasty, but the frustration of mooning over Mark Altmann all day, every day, had been interfering with her concentration on her work.

If she didn't have to look at him across the room all day, she would have been able to forget him. He was such a gorgeous-looking man, and totally unaware of it. Short cropped sandy hair, the tips bleached by the sun when he was out in the field doing research work for the museum. A beautiful—if rare—smile that lit up his face and made his eyes sparkle, and a deep melodic voice that gave her goosebumps. Even listening to Mark read out the Latin botanical names in meetings made her shiver. His formal way of speaking and the long old-fashioned words he used had been as sexy as hell.

Her daydreams at her desk had often turned those Latin words into endearments meant for her.

The happy squeals of children and splashing filled the air as Joe led her along a side verandah of the beautiful homestead. Huge grape leaves trailed from a trellis and baskets of potted colour hung from every post. It was the sort of place Leah would love to create—one day. It would be silly living in a big house by herself now. The upkeep of a house and garden would be too much work; all her time was going to be spent on making her new freelance career a success.

She could have stayed and worked in her apartment in Sydney but the happy memories of Bindarra Creek had beckoned. She'd miss her work at the museum, but she knew Mark wouldn't even notice she'd left. She hadn't been able to bring herself to tell him she was leaving when they sat next to each other at morning tea on Wednesday. She'd waited until he'd gone for the day before she packed up her desk and left the office for the last time. She drove to Bindarra Creek on Thursday and settled into a room at the Fig Tree Lodge. Edwina Lette had remembered her, and Mum and Dad.

'It's so good to see the young ones coming back home,' Edwina had said as she'd taken Leah to her room. 'Bindarra Creek is growing; there are a lot of new houses being built and the primary school numbers have gone up. There are going to be two kindy classes next year. You're not a teacher, are you, Leah? Hard to get them out here.' She looked hopeful.

'No. I'm an illustrator.'

'I always remember you being creative. We'll have to get you to help with the decorations for the Christmas carols next Saturday and the Christmas Eve picnic. Not far off now, but I'll talk to the committee.'

'I'd love to help out however I can. Christmas is my favourite time of the year.'

Leah was looking forward to the Christmas activities. This afternoon's barbeque at Joe's brother and sister-in-law's house was her first Christmas event, and she intended going to the two town festivities. It would be a good opportunity to see if there was anyone she knew still in town. She didn't need Mark Altmann to make her happy.

Foolish dreams. He didn't even know she existed.

Look ahead. Mark Altmann was in her past and she would stop thinking about him. A stupid obsession focusing on that gorgeous, clever man.

So, what are you doing now? she chastised herself.

'Are you going to all the Christmas functions in town? The carols and picnic?' she asked Joe, bringing herself back to the present.

Before he could answer, a little girl ran around the corner of the veranda and ran headfirst into Joe.

'I was, but I think I'm mortally injured now.' He bent down, picked up the little girl and swung her high in the air. 'Watch where you're going, Miss Josie. You almost knocked me off my feet.'

'Put me down, quick, Joe. I'm on a mission.'

'A mission?'

'Yes, I'm hiding from Benny,' the young girl said.

Joe put her up on his shoulders. 'He won't see you up here.'

'That's a good plan, he's too little, isn't he? Am I too heavy though?'

'What, for a strong hulk like me? I could carry three of you.'

The little girl called Josie giggled. 'You could, Joe.' On her head, she wore a red and green striped elf cap with ears on the sides, and matching striped swimmers. Silver tinsel was tied around both of her wrists.

She looked across at Leah. 'Hello, I don't know you. My name is Josie I'm going to live out near here soon. Grant's building a house for Mummy and us. Us is Billy and me, and my rooster.'

'Josie, this is Leah Maclean. She used to live in Bindarra Creek and she's come home for Christmas,' Joe said.

'Hello, Josie.' Leah said. 'It's nice to meet you.'

'You too. Is it okay if I call you Leah? Mummy always makes me check.'

'Of course. Miss Maclean makes me sound ancient.' Leah grinned up at the little girl who was full of life, but Josie's attention was distracted as a teenage boy ran around the side of the house.

'You can come back, Josie. Benny's given up on hide and seek, he wants to swim now,' he yelled.

Joe lifted Josie down and she took off with a wave at them. 'I'll get you some elf ears, Leah,' she called. 'I'll be right back. Wait here.'

Joe waited as Leah paused to admire a basket full of colourful red and white annuals. 'How Christmassy is this!'

'Jac has a green thumb. Jaclyn's my sister-in-law,' Joe said.

By the time they reached the end of the side veranda and passed a covered pergola from which the smell of roasting meat drifted, Josie was back with two elf hats the same as hers.

'I thought it would be better manners to look after you before I had a swim, Leah,' she said holding out two sets of the red and green hats. 'I got one for you too, Joe.'

Joe chuckled and took both hats from Josie, slipped one onto his head, and then tucked Leah's hair behind her ears as he slipped the other hat on her head. His eyes, when they snagged hers, held warmth and interest, and she looked away for a moment.

She was going to have to tell Joe she wasn't

looking for that sort of friend, but for the time being, she lifted her head and smiled at him.

'Thank you, Joe. And thank you, Josie. You don't know how much I love Christmas. You've made me feel very welcome.'

'Joe, Uncle Ryan needs some help in the big shed with the Weber fire thingy and he's waiting for you to help him. I even heard him say a swear word. I can take Leah over to meet Mum and Aunty Jac. Okay?'

Joe touched his hand to his forehead in a small salute. 'That okay with you, Leah?'

'That's fine. Sounds like you're needed urgently.'

As Joe left them, Josie pulled a funny face and looked quizzically at Leah. 'Are you the new girlfriend or are you just someone else he's come with? Mummy and Aunty Jac were wondering.'

Leah laughed. 'No, I'm not the new girlfriend, I'm just Joe's friend.'

'Well, I heard Aunty Jac say it's time he got one because he needs to settle down and stop playing the field.'

'How old are you, Josie?' Leah asked. She bit back a grin. 'You're very wise for your years.'

'I'm ten but I'll be eleven in October and that's not far away. And I'm really good at music already. Miss has asked me to play the triangle in the school band at the carols by candlelight next weekend. I've been practising heaps. I'm so excited. I really love Christmas. Do you?'

'I do. I love everything about Christmas, and I'll be at the carols. I'll look forward to seeing you there. Now, are you going to take me over to meet your Mum?'

By the time Josie led Leah from the veranda and across a manicured lawn to a huge undercover outdoor area beside a large inground pool, Joe was already on his way back from the shed with a beer in his hand.

'Cooking crisis averted,' he whispered as he leaned down close to her ear. His breath was warm on her cheek before he took her hand and led her across to the table.

'I'll do the honours, Josie. Hey, everyone, this is Leah Maclean. She grew up here in Bindarra Creek and she's back in town for a while.'

A man stood and walked across to where Leah stood at the end of the table with Joe.

Unusual shyness almost overcame her as everyone turned to look at her. The rugged-looking man reached out and shook her hand. 'Hi Leah, I'm Grant. Welcome. Some of us went to school here too.'

'Hello, nice to meet you, Grant.'

Joe nodded to the three women sitting at the

table. 'This is Cathy, Grant's partner.'

A pretty woman with fair hair lifted her hand with a smile. 'Hi Leah, I see Josie's already looked after you in the elf ears department.'

'She has,' Leah said with a smile, feeling a little bit more at ease. They all seemed lovely.

'And this is Cleo, and next to her is my sister-in-law, Jaclyn.'

Pretty dark curls framed dark brown eyes and the sweet smile of a very pregnant woman. 'Welcome, Leah, I'm Cleo. I think I remember you from high school. Is your last name Maclean?'

Leah nodded. 'It is.'

'You were a really good netball player,' Cleo said. 'I remember watching you play in the final against Oxley High when you were in year nine.'

'You have an excellent memory, Cleo! I do remember that game, but please excuse me if I don't remember anyone. I've been gone for ten years.'

'And we're all a bit older than you,' Cathy said with a smile.

'Hi Leah, I'm Jaclyn. What brings you back to Bindarra Creek?' The third woman smiled and gestured to the seat beside her. 'Come and sit down and satisfy our curiosity.'

'Or Josie'll have you running around with the kids,' Cathy said.

'What would you like to drink?' Grant asked. 'I've been appointed barman for the night while Ryan and Jon cook.'

'Oh, just a lime and soda, or a soft drink. Whatever's easiest,' Leah said. 'I won't be drinking. I offered to let Joe have a couple of beers and I'll drive back into town. I'll have one wine later, maybe.'

She didn't miss the look that was exchanged between Cathy and Cleo.

But Josie soon put paid to any assumptions. 'Aunty Jac, Leah isn't Joe's new girlfriend, she's just a friend, so he *can* keep playing the field. I checked.'

Cathy rolled her eyes and Leah smiled.

'Oh, Josie. Manners!' Cathy flicked an apologetic glance towards Leah. 'Sorry, Leah. We're still learning socially appropriate behaviour.'

'It's fine, and I have a lovely pair of elf ears, so everything's good.'

Rather than looking embarrassed, Jaclyn chuckled. Cleo grinned, but Cathy's cheeks stayed pink.

'I'm so pleased you're on the ball, Josie. I love your honesty,' Jaclyn said. You're certainly going to give the teachers a run around when you come to my high school, aren't you?'

'She'll have to learn a few more manners

before then,' Cathy said with a sigh.

Josie folded her arms and frowned. 'But Mummy, you always tell me to be honest.'

Cathy rolled her eyes again. 'Yes Josie, but I've also told you that you have to think about other's feelings before you speak.'

Joe laughed this time. 'Chill, Cathy, no feelings hurt here, but I'm sure you're all pleased to meet Leah.'

Leah walked around the table and took the spare seat beside Jaclyn. 'Thanks, everyone, you've made me feel very welcome, Josie included. I think I'm going to enjoy being back in Bindarra Creek.'

'Now let's tell you where we all fit in and get to know you before the hordes arrive,' Jaclyn said.

Leah leaned back in the soft chair. So far Bindarra Creek was very friendly.

Chapter 2

Sydney

Mark Altmann opened the large drawer at the bottom of his desk, barely able to contain his excitement. The email he'd been waiting for had arrived a short time ago and confirmed his hopes; he couldn't wait to tell Leah Maclean what had been sent to him. He'd printed the email out and put it in the drawer so it wasn't obvious on his always tidy, bare desk. He wanted to be the one to share the news.

Mark glanced impatiently at his watch. Leah always took the first of the two morning tea breaks at ten a.m. in the tea room at the museum, and that was still eleven minutes away. Those fifteen minutes at morning tea were the highlight of every day for him. Even if he didn't speak to her most days, he got to sit near her and watch her talk; her hands were so expressive, they moved constantly as she chatted. He guessed that it was the creative side of her that gave her the descriptive hand movements; her illustrations were the best he'd ever seen.

He would have fifteen minutes in there to

show her, and he fought to contain his excitement. Maybe she'd come over to his desk and chat with him after morning tea. She must be in a meeting upstairs because he hadn't seen her yet today, but the three floors all came down for morning tea at the same time. So, wherever she was, she'd be in the morning tea room at her usual time.

Actually—Mark glanced at his watch again—there'd be time to print the attached image out, and show Leah the photo in colour—if the colour printer was online. More often than not it was out of action, and it was almost impossible to find Rory, the IT technician when he was needed. With fingers crossed, Mark opened the email again and sent the photo to the network colour printer. He'd call in to the print room and collect the colour print on the way to morning tea.

If it was there.

Nine minutes later, Mark hesitated before he went into the lunchroom. He'd slipped a coffee bag in his cup, and he could quickly go in and top up with water from the Zip heater without having to linger in the lunchroom and be forced to have a conversation with anyone while he queued for the milk and the sugar.

There were already two of the staff from downstairs in there chatting while they made their hot drinks; he hesitated again in the doorway to let them finish, giving them a brief nod each as they passed him on the way out of the tiny kitchen.

As the hot water topped up his coffee cup and he jiggled the coffee bag before lifting it out to put in the bin, Mark froze.

Three shrill voices, all speaking together, reached him in the small space, and he cursed his bad luck as the three receptionists—one from each floor: archives, research, and communications—walked in together and filled the doorway, effectively, and perhaps not unintentionally, blocking his exit.

He'd hoped to be early enough to get his usual seat at the end of the table next to where Leah always sat, but it looked like he was out of luck today. But that wasn't going to stop him; he would show Leah what he had, no matter if he had to change his usual seat or waylay her in the corridor on their way back to the research floor after morning tea. He was going to tell her personally and he was going to work up the courage to ask her to accompany him on the research trip. He lifted his gaze from the floor, digging for courage—and normality.

Because Mark knew his shyness wasn't normal.

'Good morning, ladies. How are you today?' he managed to say.

'Hello, Mark.' Susanne from archives literally batted her eyelashes at him, and he felt the heat rise to the tips of his ears. 'How are you?'

'Can't complain. Hello, Rhonda. Hi . . . um . . . Alisa, how are you?' Mark could feel the perspiration building. 'How's work down on your floors this week?'

'Busy as usual, but I'm pleased it's Friday.' Alisa said, and to his relief, the three turned their attention to making coffee.

Mark put the coffee bag in the kitchen bin and waited for them to step aside for him to leave the kitchen, their giggling following him as he made his way to his usual seat. His confidence built; he'd got out of that pretty easily. It was strange; talking to Leah never stressed him like that. He sat down, surprised she wasn't already in her seat. She was always very punctual, another trait he admired about her. Not to mention her vivacious personality *and* her pretty eyes.

No matter what mood Leah was in, no matter what the day had brought at the museum—and he knew some of them could be super hard when the work came in all at once, plus some of the days could be very exciting as new discoveries and disappointments surfaced, and that always tended to create the moods on each floor. Leah was always positive and had a ready smile for him—and everyone else. Sometimes Mark kidded himself that her smile was just for him, but he always woke up to himself in time before he could make a fool of himself by asking her out.

Maybe one day.

Maybe they could get to know each other better on a research trip.

He chose his usual seat next to where she always sat and leaned back on the vinyl chair, putting his coffee mug on the table to cool. Hopefully, she'd be here soon; she had taken the day off yesterday and the office had been empty without her.

Herman Holgate from the archives section on the ground floor walked in carrying his ready-made cup of tea, made for him each tea break by his secretary. None of that sort of attention for the top two floors of the museum.

'Morning, Mark,' Herman's deep voice boomed, causing another round of giggles from the receptionists in the kitchen. 'Everything going to plan this week?'

Mark schooled his features into a normal expression. He wasn't going to tell Herman about the email yet.

In fact, he wasn't going to tell anybody. Leah deserved to know first; she was the one who'd done the incredible drawings from the one blurred photo he had and sent them out to all the national parks and local councils for him.

So, she alone could take credit for the success in locating the plant that he'd been seeking for several years. Perhaps it was an omen that the rare native mistletoe had surfaced at Christmas time. Perhaps it *was* time he asked Leah out.

Mark's confidence built as he anticipated her arrival and her delight in seeing his success. *Their* success. He would suggest a drink after work to celebrate.

Yes, that was an excellent plan. He sat still, trying to think of a secluded bar near the museum. He never went out, so he would have to ask. Maybe the girls in the kitchen?

But his dilemma was, he didn't want anyone to know what he planned. And if it was a bar they suggested, there was a chance that they would be there too.

No, not a good idea at all.

'Mark?' Herman's voice was loud. 'I asked have you had a good week up there?'

Mark brought himself back to the present and nodded. 'Yes. Yes, I have. How about you, Herman?'

Herman nodded. 'Yes, I've spent most of the day drafting an ad. It's going to be hard to replace someone of Leah's calibre, but she was immovable. Refused to discuss staying, and I probably shouldn't tell you, but she even missed out on her holiday pay by leaving before the museum closes for Christmas.'

Mark knew his eyes were wide and he tried to keep his tone normal. 'Replace Leah? Immovable? What have I missed?'

'I even offered her a pay rise, but she wouldn't budge. Aren't you aware she left the museum on Wednesday?'

'Left? Left, as in left her position? Not just for a day off?'

'Yes, she's left the museum and is going into this silly freelance business. Damn waste, if you ask me. She's not going to make a living. I was just reading a report about freelancing in Australia. She would be much better staying here on a salary.'

'Freelance in what? Natural illustration?' Mark finally found his voice.

'No, silly drawings or some such thing for children's books,' Herman said. 'Typical female, can't depend on any of them, Mark. Three divorces have taught me that.'

Mark didn't comment. He had always found Leah to be extremely reliable, very even-tempered and amenable to any last-minute work.

He'd been deceiving himself all along, thinking that she'd liked him. In fact, he'd hoped that she more than liked him, and had occasionally suspected a faint reciprocation of the attraction that he held for her, but Mark had never been able to summon up the courage to ask her out.

He'd been way off track; he'd simply been somebody else that she cooperated with in the workplace. She hadn't even thought highly enough of him to let him know that she was leaving and going off to another position.

Mark reached out for his coffee and grasped the mug, letting the warmth of the coffee mug in his hand ease the cold in his heart.

Chapter 3

Jaclyn and Ryan's Christmas Barbeque

Dinner had been cleared away, and children were snuggling in their parents' arms as a curtain of soft darkness stole over the landscape and the first stars appeared in the magical sky. It seemed as though the entire town had come to Ryan and Jaclyn's place for the Christmas barbeque. Leah sat back in her chair drawing breath as contentment and peace filled her; it had amazed her how many people had remembered her from school.

Joe had gone across to the house to help Ryan put the leftover meat away before he and Leah headed back to town. She was driving his car to the pub where they'd met. Apparently, the night promised to be a big one, and Joe tried to talk her into coming back to the pub with him.

She looked up with a smile as Grant sat beside her.

'Joe told me you might be looking for somewhere to live after Christmas?'

'After the lovely welcome I received tonight, I think that's a strong possibility,' she replied.

'It certainly is a great little town,' Grant said. 'I had no intention of staying when I came back a few months ago, but now I have an instant family, and Cathy and I are building a house just up the road.'

Leah smiled. 'I can't see that happening to me, but I'm pretty sure I'll stay for a while. Will your duplex be available soon? I'm only at Fig Tree Lodge until New Year's Day.'

'Come and have a look at it tomorrow and see if it suits you. I'm sure we can work something out. We're moving into a rental house with a bit of land so there's more room for the kids.'

'Just about ready, Leah?' Joe had joined them while she and Grant were talking.

Leah stood. 'I am.'

'Watch out for the roos on the way back to town. They'll be out and about tonight,' Grant warned.

'I will. I'll just say thanks to Ryan and Jac, and goodbye to Cathy and Cleo. I'll meet you at the car if you like, Joe.'

Half an hour later, Leah parked Joe's work ute in the last vacant parking spot of the Riverside Pub. He'd been very persuasive on the drive back to town and had talked her into coming in for a drink.

'Just one,' she'd agreed.

'Two. And then I'll walk you back to Fig Tree Lodge. The pub will be hopping. A lot of locals are back in town for Christmas.'

'I can walk back myself,' Leah insisted.

'No. I'll walk you home. I certainly wouldn't want you wandering around Bindarra Creek by yourself at night.'

'Joe, I'll be fine. I've wandered around the eastern suburbs of Sydney by myself for the past six years. I'd catch the bus home from the city and then walk six blocks to my apartment.'

'We've had a few nasty things happen in town the last few months. I'd feel much better if you let me take you home.' Joe looked at her curiously as they got out of the ute at the pub. 'Didn't you ever have a fella to look after you in the big smoke?' He moved closer and Leah took a step back, shaking her head.

'I can look after myself.'

'I like you, Leah,' Joe said slowly. 'I'd like to get to know you better.'

'And I like you too, Joe, but I'm not in the market for a relationship. I came here to get over a bruised—I won't say broken—heart.'

'Okay. But I'll still walk you home.' He held his hands up. 'No strings attached, honest.'

'Thank you. I'll accept graciously.'

Chapter 4
Riverside Pub

Joe found them a table over near the door that led to the back deck of the pub.

'It'd be nicer outside,' he said. 'But everyone's headed for the deck tonight. There's a great view of the river and the kids play on the lawn out there.'

'It's fine in here.' Leah looked around as Joe headed over to the bar to get their drinks. Her gaze was drawn to a man sitting at a table on the other side of the doorway. She stared, blinked and then as she stared again, her heart began an erratic beat.

'Oh my God.' Leah's thoughts were at a screech level in her head as she clenched her hands in her lap.

'Oh my God. Oh my God. *Oh. My. God.*' Her lips moved silently as she stared across the room. Blood fizzed through her veins and her body heated, as though she'd been drinking all night even though she'd only had one wine at Ryan and Jac's place two hours ago. She felt almost giddy-drunk with excitement.

Oh my God. He had followed her. In her

daydreams, Leah had imagined Mark being distraught when he found out she'd left and that he would come looking for her when he realised that he couldn't live without her. She had laughed at herself on the drive up, telling herself what a ridiculous scenario that was, and that Mark Altmann would no longer stay in her thoughts . . . or her heart.

He had followed her.

Mark Altmann had followed her to Bindarra Creek only two days after she'd left the city. A huge smile spread across Leah's face as happiness surged through her. Her departure had made him show his hand, and she was so thankful that she'd decided to leave the museum. The move had been a great idea.

She could not believe Mark Altmann had followed her all the way to Bindarra Creek.

'Okay,' she said to herself. 'How am I going to handle this? Will I go and tell him I've seen him, or will I wait until he finds me?'

The thought that Mark had left Sydney and come all the way to Bindarra Creek to find her was unbelievable. He *had* known how she felt about him, and he reciprocated that feeling.

Leah had wondered about that a couple of times over the past six months when she'd caught him looking at her in the same way she looked at him when she knew he wasn't watching. But she'd put it down to a foolish hope.

But never once had he given any indication by his words or actions that he was interested in her too.

But now, here he was, he'd followed her to her hometown, so he had to feel the same way she did. Had he come to beg her to come back? Or to talk to her? Or to ask her out? To tell her that he loved her?

What was the best opening line? What was the best way to greet him? Something witty, with a sexy look.

Leah panicked. She hadn't looked in a mirror since she'd left Figtree Lodge this afternoon. Maybe she could head to the ladies without him spotting her, and check that her hair was okay and she didn't have tomato sauce on her face.

Oh, my God. She watched him as he sat at a table with his head down, looking at his phone.

Maybe he was looking for her number. Maybe he'd tried to call already. She hadn't taken her phone out to the Rossiter's farm; it was still on the antique cabinet beside the four-poster bed in her room at the lovely old lodge.

Maybe I should go home and get it?

Don't be stupid, she chastised herself. If he's trying to ring you or if he's already tried to ring you, you might as well just get up and go over and talk to him, silly girl.

'Oh my God,' she muttered again.

'Are you okay, Leah?'

She jumped and looked up, but it was Joe, standing there with a drink in each hand and a worried look on his face.

'Yes, I am. No, I'm not. Yes, I sort of am, but I'm not. Why do you ask?'

'Your face is all red, and you look terrified. Is everything okay?' He looked around as if to see if anyone had bothered her.

'Yes, very okay. Joe, look, thanks for the drink, but there's someone here I need to see. I hope that's okay. Actually—' she picked the glass of wine and sculled it in one hit— 'I need some Dutch courage. Thanks for taking me out to the farm. And thanks for a great evening. There's someone here I need to go and see. Someone special. I'll see you around. Okay, thank you.'

Joe looked bemused as she jumped to her feet and kissed his cheek.

'It was a lovely evening, and I think it's about to get even better,' she said.

Before Leah could stop herself, her shaking legs propelled her over to the table where Mark Altmann was still focused on his phone. She let her eyes drink him in as she approached.

Mark's black T-shirt fit him snugly; she

hadn't really noticed his build in the loose shirts he wore in the office. The fit of this shirt showed off broad shoulders and muscular arms.

Oh, be still my beating heart.

A warm feeling headed south, and she bit her lip.

Too soon, too soon. Take it slow, girl.

It would hardly be appropriate to plaster herself against that gorgeous body before they even talked. No matter how much her hormones cried out for her to fling her arms around him and press herself against that gorgeous man.

'Act properly,' she told herself as she kept her eyes on him. 'Be sensible, but sophisticated.' She lifted her hands and ran her fingers through her loose, long hair. She froze as her fingers encountered the striped elf ears on her head.

Sophisticated, not!

But it was too late to take them off. With a deep shaky breath, Leah took the final two steps to the table and stood there waiting for Mark to notice her, but it was a full minute before he looked up. She tried to say his name, but her mouth was dry.

When he did look up, just as she was licking her dry lips, a smile tilted his mouth, but strangely, the smile disappeared as quickly as it had come.

'Mark,' she said breathlessly. 'I am just so

pleased. I am so, so happy to see you here.' Her voice was husky, but she guessed that sounded sexy rather than nervous.

He rose to his feet like the gentleman he was, leaving his phone on the table.

'You're pleased? I'm extremely pleased to see you here. Having you here with your skills will make all the difference,' he said. 'How did you know that I'd come out here?'

'I always held hope,' she said and paused when he frowned.

'Hope?' he repeated. 'Did Herman ring you? Although I don't know how he found out about it, unless he was copied into the email.'

Leah frowned. Why on earth would he email silly Herman Holgate about following her to Bindarra Creek?

'Email? Did you email me or did you try to call? I haven't got my phone with me. And found out about what?'

His glance flicked away from her briefly and over towards his phone. 'No, I didn't. How did you know where to find me?' he said.

What? How did I know where to find him?

For a moment, Leah frowned, wondering why they seemed to be talking at sixes and sevens. 'I didn't know where to find you,' she said hesitantly. 'I was just ecstat— I mean I was pleased when I saw you sitting there. To know that you've come out here to . . . to look for . . .'

Me! she thought as he interrupted.

'To look for the elusive native mistletoe,' he said.

Leah's jaw dropped as her heart plummeted, and her blood seemed to flow sluggishly through her body. 'What? What did you say?'

'The native mistletoe, the one that I've been searching for. You know it, Leah. I mean you've drawn it for me how many times over the last three years?'

Leah swallowed, unsure of what was going on. Maybe she was having trouble understanding because she'd sculled that drink. 'May I sit with you,' she asked tentatively.

'Of course. How rude of me. Please sit.' Mark pulled out the chair beside his. She glanced at it and then chose the one on the other side of the table. Leah was starting to see she had been awfully, awfully wrong.

'Now tell me exactly why you're in Bindarra Creek. Did you know I was here?' she asked slowly.

Mark's eyes held hers and the usual rush of pleasure consumed her, but she ignored it. She was only hot because it was hot inside the pub.

'Did *you* know I was here?' he asked, not taking his eyes off hers.

Those warm shivers ran down to where her hands were now clenched in her lap. Did Mark know what effect his voice alone had on her? If he ever touched her, she would sizzle up.

'No. I didn't.'

She thought a flicker of disappointment crossed his face, but it was too dim in this corner to see clearly, and her head was spinning from sculling that drink.

His voice wasn't as warm now. 'So, what are you doing in Bindarra Creek, Leah?' The excitement in his eyes had lessened as he continued to regard her intently. The sweet shivers stopped, replaced by cold realisation.

'Because I'm moving here,' she said. 'This is where I grew up. Why are *you* here?'

She hoped and hoped that he would say because he had followed her here, but she already knew in her heart that wasn't the case.

'I'm in Bindarra Creek because there's been a sighting of the rare mistletoe. Isn't that fantastic!'

'Oh,' she said quietly, knowing that she had just stopped talking in time. A few seconds later if she'd kept going, she would have made an almighty fool of herself. It was just an awful coincidence.

'Well,' he said briskly. 'I know you don't

work for the museum anymore, but perhaps you could come out into the field with me and draw what we hopefully find?'

***

'How could I have ever thought that Leah Maclean had followed me out to the bush?' Mark chastised himself.

She'd left the museum without even telling him, and the instant he saw her, he'd foolishly thought that she'd heard about him coming here and had dropped everything and followed him out. He had gone so close to saying he'd assumed that; thank goodness he'd held back. She probably would have laughed in his face.

Once Mark had decided to head out to the Akuna National Park and find the site of the elusive native mistletoe, he had been packed and, on the road west within six hours. If he'd been thinking straight when Leah had appeared at the table, he would have realised that there was no way she could have followed him out so quickly.

There had been no point hanging around. The museum had now closed until after the New Year, and he hated the thought of staying in the city and having to go to a never-ending round of family Christmas dinners. He'd called in at the local pharmacy, bought a gift pack for his mother and then stopped at the bottle shop and picked up a bottle of spiced rum for his dad, had them both gift-wrapped and left them under the Christmas tree with a note saying he was going out of town for work.

It might have been cowardly, but he didn't want to see the disappointment on Mum's face.

Again.

At the last minute, he realised he hadn't thought of accommodation being booked out at Christmas so he threw his swag in the back of his Jeep just in case. The national park where the mistletoe had been spotted was just outside a small country town, and he was pretty hopeful, he'd pick up a room at a pub or similar.

He'd arrived at the local caravan park, paid for an unpowered site and headed to the pub on the river for dinner. He'd been rereading his notes on his phone when something had made him look up.

When he looked up and saw Leah standing at the table looking down at him, disbelief filled him. His first instinct had been to jump up and put his arms around her. She looked absolutely beautiful even with that silly Christmas hat on her head.

He had forced his arms to stay by his side and closed down the goofy smile on his face. He couldn't believe how close he'd gone to making an absolute fool of himself.

He'd honestly thought that Leah had heard he was out here looking for the native mistletoe and that she'd followed him all the way to Bindarra Creek to help him. The Christmas hat should have been an instant giveaway but he hadn't been thinking straight.

What were the chances of such a coincidence? The chances of her being here. How many national parks were in New South Wales? He couldn't believe Leah had moved here from Sydney. He had no idea what this freelancing business was about and all he *should* have been thinking about was what a waste it was, her moving here. He *should* have been thinking about what an asset she had been to the museum and to his work.

But as their gazes met and held, all Mark could think was how beautiful she was. Leah's lips were parted softly, and her cheeks were a pretty pink. She lifted her hand and removed the elf hat from her head as her green eyes stayed on his.

'They looked cute,' he said before he could help it.

Cute? He'd never used that word before in his life.

'What?'

'The ears. They're cute.'

'They were just something silly. I know how much you hate Christmas frivolity, Mark. I was at a

Christmas function with my friend, Joe.' She gestured to a huge man watching them curiously from the bar. Mark noticed he wore ears too.

'So, tell me why you're here and tell me what you're planning,' Leah said briskly.

'Firstly, would you like a drink,' he asked.

'Why not?' She stared at him for a moment, her voice holding an unusual tone.

Hardness?

Disappointment?

Embarrassment?

'Um, er, what do you like to drink, Leah? The only thing I've ever seen you drink is a cup of tea.'

'White wine would be fine, thank you. A big one.'

Mark walked over to the bar; the big man wearing the elf hat was looking at him strangely.

'Two glasses of white wine, please,' he asked the barman. As he waited the man left his stool and moved closer to Mark.

'Do you know Leah?' he asked immediately.

Mark stood straight. He was well over six feet tall, but he had to look up to this guy. 'I do. Is that a problem?' Unfamiliar belligerence took hold.

'No. Only if you hurt her. She looked upset when she saw you there.'

'No, not at all, I wouldn't hurt her for the world,' Mark said. 'We were work colleagues in Sydney. I think Leah did get a surprise to see me, however.'

The guy held his hand out and Mark took it.

'Mark Altmann.'

His grip was crushing as he shook, and Mark suspected there was a warning in it.

'I'm Joe Rossiter.' His eyes narrowed. 'Just take care of her. Okay?' He picked up his beer and walked back to his stool, the elf ears waggling.

Mark paid for the wines and crossed the pub back to where Leah was sitting at his table. What a strange thing for Joe to say to him.

Just take care of her?

Maybe Leah had personal reasons for leaving the museum that she hadn't told Herman. Maybe he should ask her if she was all right. Perhaps it had been presumptuous of him to ask her to help him search for the elusive native plant.

As he walked across to the table, the truth hit him.

The only reason a man would say that to him was if he thought Mark was involved with Leah. Much as he would've liked that very much, Mark knew Leah would never look at him in that way.

She was sitting quietly with her hands

folded in her lap.

'Here we go,' he said putting her glass of wine carefully on a coaster.

'Thank you,' she said formally. Any hint of warmth was gone, and he had second thoughts about telling her of his research plans.

Leah's usual vivacity and joy of life seem to have disappeared and he wondered why?

He glanced back over to the bar. Joe was sitting on a stool, shooting an occasional frosty glance their way, and Mark wondered if perhaps that was why Leah had moved here. Maybe they were in a relationship? That would explain Joe's attitude. Mark almost laughed; he'd reached the ripe old age of thirty-five and had never been considered a threat before.

He didn't know how to begin, so he held up his glass. 'Merry Christmas, Leah,' he said.

Chapter 5

While Mark was at the bar getting their drinks, Leah tried to compose herself. She put her head down and closed her eyes, focusing on her breathing. She was kidding herself if she thought she could get over him; no matter how much she wanted to, there was something that kept telling her he was the right man for her.

After all, she'd worked with him for six years, and had never once let her control slip, and the feelings she had for him had developed slowly over that time. She had always been professional, and all of her dreams had stayed in her head. Never once had she shown him what she was thinking; she was just being a silly, immature teenager like she'd been at high school. Because that was what they were. Dreams.

Only dreams.

That was why she'd left. She'd had visions of herself, grey and wrinkled, working at the museum, and still mooning over Mark.

They were professional colleagues, and that's what she had to keep foremost in her mind and ignore those blasted shivers and the butterflies that had gone crazy in her lower belly.

He was a *colleague*.

By the time he came back with the drinks, she had composed herself.

When he picked up his glass and waited for her to clink glasses, and wished her Merry Christmas, her eyebrows lifted in surprise.

She was very pleased with how calm her voice was. 'Merry Christmas, Mark. I didn't think you liked Christmas.'

He seemed to relax as he sipped his wine. 'Caused by my mother's overwhelming over-the-top appreciation of the festive season. Would you believe it's only been a couple of years since my brother and I were excused from decorating the Christmas tree?'

'Is your brother a lot younger than you?' She choked on her wine. 'Ah, not saying that I think you're old.'

'No. He's thirty-seven and he finally stood Mum up. He works in Canberra and she expected him to make a special trip home the first weekend in December to do the tree. So, you can see why I am less than enthusiastic when the tinsel appears and the carols are piped over the floors at work.'

Leah's interest stirred. In all the years she'd known him, he had never once talked about anything other than work.

'Your mother sounds as though she values family.'

'She does, but I draw the line at all the Christmas visits with my parents That's why when the email arrived about the *Loranthus tetrapetalus* it gave me the perfect excuse to leave home for the festive season.'

'What did she say?'

Mark's smile sent those butterflies swirling in her tummy. 'I was a coward. I left a note and their presents under the Christmas tree and I fled. Yes, I regret to confess that a man of my age still lives at home with his parents.'

She smiled and noticed the tips of his ears colour to a dark pink. 'I don't see anything wrong with that.'

'But you're surprised?'

Her smile grew as her enjoyment of the conversation grew. 'I didn't think you ever went home from the museum. I thought you were like that guy in that museum movie and you stayed there all night.'

That warm smile lifted his full lips. No man should be allowed to have such a beautiful mouth.

'No, I do have a home living with my parents. But I have an independent flat beneath the back of the house so it's not as though I'm still in my teenage bedroom. I can go all week without seeing them. What about you?' he asked. 'Is your family still in Sydney?' His brow wrinkled in a frown. 'Or do they live here? Is that why you came to Bindarra Creek?'

'No. Mum and Dad live in Brisbane now. I came to Bindarra Creek because I had such a great time growing up here, and I thought this would be a nice place to start my new career. A place to get the creative juices flowing.'

'Herman did mention something briefly about a new career. What are you doing, Leah?'

'I'm going to illustrate children's books,' she said.

'I think you'd be very good at that, but I thought you quite enjoyed your work at the museum.' Mark's brow wrinkled again in that same frown and she looked down. Even with a frown on his face, the man was damnably good-looking. There should be a law against anyone having such perfect looks.

'Yes, I did, but shall we say circumstances made it difficult to keep working there.'

He shot a glance over at Joe, who was leaning back on the bar occasionally looking their way.

'Yes, I understand why it would be difficult to have a relationship at such a long distance.'

'A relationship?' Leah frowned this time

and then the penny dropped as Mark glanced across to the bar.

'Ah,' she said without agreeing or disagreeing. A supposed relationship with Joe! That's exactly what she needed Mark to think, and it would save her any embarrassment if she ever let anything slip. She wasn't going to lie to him, but she could use clever words.

'Yes, Bindarra Creek is a long way from Sydney. Now enough about me. Tell me what has happened here, Mark.'

Leah was very proud of the way she was keeping herself together. If she didn't catch those mesmerising hazel eyes again, she could stay composed. It was just that when she caught his gaze on her and she held it, her heart rate took off. That was when she knew she was in trouble. The incredible thing was that Mark seemed totally unaware of the impact he had on her. She was sure he had no idea how sexy he was.

His gold-flecked hazel eyes were surrounded by long, dark eyelashes that any woman would sell her soul for.

She needed to protect her heart until he left town and went back to the museum. Then she could focus on Bindarra Creek and forget about him.

And pigs might fly, said the little voice in her head.

If Mark believed she and Joe were seeing each other that would give her an out while he was in town.

But is that fair to Joe?

Maybe if she told him what was going on, he'd be happy to pretend.

But isn't that rude to use someone you barely know?

Someone who was interested in a relationship.

Leah put her glass down on the coaster and stood. 'Please excuse me for a moment. Then you can tell me all about the mistletoe and what you need me to do.'

Before Mark could speak, she left the table and headed to the ladies. It would look a bit rude heading straight over to Joe, so she'd visit the ladies, make a detour on the way back and run her proposal by Joe.

Leah pushed open the door to the ladies' room and almost knocked over a short, plump woman with brown curly hair who was on her way out. They both squealed at the same time.

'Leah!' said the other woman.

'Mandy!' Leah exclaimed. 'Oh my gosh, Mandy Kaminsky, how good to see you.' She grabbed Mandy's hands. 'Are you still Kaminsky or married?'

'Still Kaminsky. Oh wow, Leah. You've come home for Christmas. I haven't seen you for over ten years. What about you? Still Maclean? You don't look any different from high school.'

'Neither do you.'

Mandy chuckled. 'I was always short and plump!'

'You were always gorgeous and you still are. Oh, it's so good to see another familiar face. I haven't been back since I left to go to university. What about you?'

'I came home about four years ago,' Mandy said. 'I'm in the Fire Service and I've got a part-time job as a teachers' aide at the primary school. You're not a teacher these days are you, Leah? We really need new staff at both schools. There are so many people moving to Bindarra Creek—new and returnees—the town's growing quickly. It's fabulous to see.'

Leah chuckled. 'Edwina has already run that by me and no, the best thing I can do for children is draw pictures for their picture books. I'm an illustrator and I think I'm moving back here to stay, so it's so wonderful to find out that you still live here.'

Leah was really excited to hear Mandy was back in town. They'd been great mates in year nine before Mandy had moved away at the beginning of year ten, and then Leah had become friends with Natalie and Ruth. She and Mandy had corresponded by email for a couple of years and then in the usual way of things they had lost contact.

'It's so good to see you. Do you want to come outside and sit with me?' Mandy asked.

'A few of us from the "firies" are having an early Christmas drink. But you're probably here with someone.'

Leah couldn't help rolling her eyes. She and Mandy had shared all of their teenage dreams. She shook her head. 'You wouldn't believe it. I came in here to sort out my thoughts. I came to Bindarra Creek to sort out my life, and would you believe that the guy that I was trying to get away from has turned up here in town on a work-related thing? An absolute coincidence.'

'Are you sure it was?'

'Yes, Mark was as surprised to see me as I was to see him. I can do with a bit of female advice if you want to help me out. I've just been out to a barbeque at the Rossiter's farm with Joe Rossiter.'

'Now that is one gorgeous hunk of a man,' Mandy said, waggling her eyebrows.

'He's a nice guy too. I met him here at the pub the other night. And I know he's sort of interested and that's what's stopping me. I was going to ask him to pretend to be my boyfriend so

Mark would think that's why I left Sydney.'

'This sounds a bit complicated. You don't like this Mark guy?'

'Oh, I do, I've been half in love with him for years, but he doesn't even know I exist.'

'So, why's he out here?'

'It's a long story.'

'You'd better tell me the short version. And remember what a romantic I am.'

Leah laughed. 'You always did cut to the chase. I remember you and your soppy movies. Actually, it's a quick story. A case of unrequited love. That's why I'm home, to forget about him!'

'Are you sure it's unrequited?'

'He is totally immersed in his work and he's not interested in me at all.'

'Is he gay?' Mandy asked.

'I don't know anything about him,' Leah said. 'I've only just found out five minutes ago he still lives with his mum and dad in the flat under their house in Sydney. We worked together for years, and we've never had a personal conversation even though we've sat next to each other every morning tea break, and talked about work. I've slowly fallen for him a little bit more each day.'

'I've got to check this guy out,' Mandy said. 'And you reckon Joe is interested in you?'

'I shouldn't really say that. We spent a night

here chatting at the pub on Thursday night when we met, and then he asked me out to Jac and Ryan's place today for a barbecue.' Leah sighed. 'When he said he would like to see me a little bit more I told Joe I wasn't interested in a relationship. And then when Mark went to the bar to get our drinks, I noticed Joe spoke to him. I don't know what he said.'

'So,' Mandy said. 'The bottom line is, you've got the hots for someone, he's not reciprocating, and you were thinking about using Joe to put him off the scent.'

Leah grinned and nodded. 'In a nutshell.'

'I can totally sympathise,' Mandy said. 'I had the hots for someone in town here for a long time too, but he got married. We need to get together and have a drink.'

'It's a date.'

'Where are you staying?' Mandy asked.

'At Fig Tree Lodge but I'm going to have a look at a duplex tomorrow. What about you?

'I've got a flat over in Court Street. Are you free for dinner tomorrow night?'

'I am. Here?'

I'll meet you at seven.'

'And thanks, Mandy. It *would* be mean to use Joe like that. I just have to be a big girl and cope with Mark being here. I'll just have to hide how I feel and be super professional.'

'I'm sure you can do it. I'll see you tomorrow night.'

They quickly exchanged phone numbers and shared a hug before Mandy left and Leah headed to the basin. She stood in front of the mirror, ran her fingers through her hair and pinched her cheeks, surprised to see she looked relatively normal, despite her churning emotions.

Pushing open the door, she caught Mark's eye immediately. He must have been watching the door. She flicked her hands to dry them, tucked her hair behind her ears, and put a smile on her face. As she passed the bar, Joe nodded at her and she smiled back.

'Sorry I was so long. I bumped into an old friend in the ladies,' she apologised. 'Now tell me all about this sighting. And tell me what you'd like me to do.' Leah knew well what she would like, but she reminded herself sternly this was business.

Excitement filled his expression and his eyes sparkled. She could have sworn the gold flecks were glinting.

Those blasted butterflies started fluttering again.

'Okay, to start at the beginning, I got an email on Thursday about the mistletoe.' Mark took out his phone and gestured to the chair beside her.

'May I come and sit there next to you?'

She shrugged. 'Why not?'

When he joined her the bitter-sweet fragrance of his citrus aftershave surrounded her.

Give me strength.

Mark put his phone on the table and leaned forward as he flicked through his Google photos. Leah couldn't help the exclamation that burst from her as his screen filled with one of the photos. A close-up of the red flower.

'Oh, my goodness, it really is, isn't it?'

Mark nodded and grinned. His arm brushed hers as he put his finger on the phone again to flick through more photos.

'I know it so well, I've drawn it so many times,' Leah said. 'Those twin leaves could draw themselves now.'

'It certainly looks like it. It's identical to your drawing, isn't it.'

Leah took a deep breath. 'It is and you say it's out here at Bindarra Creek? I can't believe it.'

'Yes, out in the Akuna National Park according to my source who sent the photo. He said that the person who took the photo said it was about four kilometres along the track and then about two hundred metres east in a stand of *xanthorrhoea johnsonii.*'

'That's grass trees from memory?' Leah

focused on the background of the shot. She could just see the black bark of the tree. She was focusing on something other than Mark for the first time since she'd seen him in the pub. And it felt good.

'Well, what are you waiting for?' she asked, meeting his eyes, unable to hold back her happy grin.

'I was waiting to find a local photographer who would come out with me, but now I have something even better.'

Leah frowned. 'Your own camera?'

'No, my own illustrator. Would you come out with me tomorrow, Leah?'

Without hesitation, she agreed. 'Of course I will.' It would be incredible to be there when he identified the rare plant.

'There is one problem, but with your local knowledge we might overcome it to a certain extent.'

'A problem?'

'Yes. The gentleman who took the photo described the distances of the tracks, but he didn't specify which track. I've downloaded the National Park maps onto my phone and it appears there are several possibilities. Many tracks go for more than four kilometres and the guy who gave me the photo has no idea which track his contact was on.'

'Well, I guess we better try them all,' she

said. 'Although I can probably remember where some of the grass trees were. I spent a lot of time hiking out in the national park in my teens.'

Mark's face lit up. 'That's great.'

'I've got some ownership in this search, boyo. I spent hours and hours drawing those flowers for you. Plus, I think it'll be pretty cool to see what is actually going on in the wild and be there when you find it. It'll be the first sighting in Australia. You'll be famous.'

'*If* we find it,' he said.

'Okay, if we find it.' Leah picked up her glass and drank the rest of her wine. 'It's time that I went home and got some sleep. I've had a big day. Did you drive out here today, Mark?'

'I did.'

'You're probably tired too.'

'Yes, I am a bit, but more excited though. I'll probably go back and do some work before the—' He pulled a face. 'I forgot. My phone is nearly flat. So, I won't be able to hotspot my laptop.'

'Where are you staying? Can't you charge it there?'

'I'm in my swag on an unpowered site in the caravan park.'

For a very brief moment, Leah thought of inviting Mark back to her room to use the power point.

Bad idea.

'What about your car? Can't you charge it in there?'

'Good thinking. When I get back, I'll drive around for a while.'

'But promise, no going out to the national park without me.'

'I promise. We'll go together. So, how about I collect you in the morning at about eight thirty?' he asked. 'Does that suit?'

'That sounds good. I'm staying at a place called Fig Tree Lodge. It's only a couple of blocks from here.'

'I noticed that lodge when I walked down to the pub for tea. It's a beautiful building. Looks like it would have some history.'

'Oh, it does. You'll have to meet Edwina Lette and get her to tell you. It's supposed to be haunted too.'

'Do you have a car here?' Mark asked.

'No. I drove Joe, so he could have a drink and I'm walking home.'

'Shall I walk you home?' he asked hesitantly, back to the old shy Mark. When they'd been talking about the mistletoe, he had been full of a new confidence.

'I guess as you're walking that way, you can

walk home with me.'

'What about . . .' His eyes flicked over to Joe who was now in a group next to the bar.

'Joe? No. He'll be staying here for a while, I would say, with his mates and then he's going to walk home too.'

Mark pushed his half-full glass to the middle of the table.

'You haven't finished your drink yet,' Leah said. 'I'm happy to sit here for a while longer.'

'No, it's fine I'm not much of a drinker. It was a bit sour.'

Leah giggled. 'No, it's not, I guess you bought the house wine. I didn't like to say anything. Usually Chateau de Cardboard here.'

Mark grinned. 'In fact, it was really awful. I nearly gagged when you drank yours before. I haven't heard of that one. Is it a local vineyard?'

Leah's laugh was loud and a couple of heads, including Joe's, turned their way.

'No, silly. It means it's cask wine.'

He shook his head. 'None the wiser.'

'You don't know what cask wine is? What did you drink in your teens?'

'I didn't.'

'You know? A cardboard box with one of those shiny foil bags inside with a tap on the outside.'

He shook his head. 'I don't think I've ever seen one.'

'You haven't missed out on anything.'

As they walked across the room and headed towards the side door, Leah put her hand on his arm. 'Can you just wait a moment for me, please? I'll let Joe know I've got company to take me home. He was worried about me walking by myself. He reckons the town's a bit dangerous.'

'You find danger everywhere,' Mark said. 'Even in quiet sleepy towns.'

Leah nodded and walked across to Joe. 'Thanks for a lovely afternoon, Joe. I just wanted you to know that I'm going home now.'

Joe put the schooner glass he was holding on the bar. 'I'll walk you home. I said I would.'

'There's no need,' she said. 'Mark's staying at the caravan park and he has to go that way, so he's offered to walk me home.'

Joe's eyes were very aware. 'And I think that you might be quite happy about that.'

'You could be right, or you could be wrong. I'm a bit tired of people second-guessing me tonight.' Leah reached up and kissed Joe's cheek. 'Thank you again for a lovely day. I'm sure I'll see you around somewhere over Christmas.'

'You will. I'll unlock the car from here so you can get your bag out.'

'Thank you.'

She knew Joe's eyes followed her as she went out to catch up to Mark.

Chapter 6

Mark waited on the veranda at the side of the pub until Leah came out; she was smiling when she joined him and he pushed away the little tug of jealousy that surfaced. He had no right to be jealous of another man's interest in Leah Maclean.

'Right to go?' he asked.

'I am. Joe's car is unlocked. I just have to get my bag out of it.'

'You're trusting. You weren't worried about it being stolen?'

'It hasn't been unlocked all night. He just clicked the remote so I could get my stuff.' Leah opened the passenger door and reached over to the floor and pulled out a small handbag and a padded cooler bag.

Mark held out his hand for the cooler. 'Let me carry that for you.'

'It's not heavy.'

'I insist.'

She passed it to him with that delicate shrug of her shoulders Mark had become used to when they worked together. They walked two blocks towards the main street and then Leah indicated that they turn left. As they walked towards the next corner, voices and laughter reached them from a shop that was lit up with Christmas lights around the large window.

'Looks like there's a Christmas party at the Cyprus Café too,' Leah said. 'We turn right here and Fig Tree Lodge is on the next corner.'

After they turned into the next street, they left the noise behind them and the street was deserted.

'It's very quiet here, isn't it?' he commented, stating the obvious and immediately feeling silly. His brain went to mush when Leah was around him.

'It's a quiet town,' she replied. 'It's what I liked about it when I lived here. It's all I could think of when I decided to come back, and in two days it hasn't disappointed me. But you watch this time next Saturday night, the Christmas carols will be on, and people will come from far and wide. I remember them when I was growing up. Everyone brings a picnic rug or a camp chair and listens to the carols. This year the school band's going to play. Josie, a young friend of mine, is playing the triangle and she's really excited. You will come, won't you?'

'That's a week away, Leah. I don't know that I'll even be in town.'

'But you said you weren't going home for Christmas. Where else will you go?'

He hesitated. 'I don't know yet.' Mark didn't know if he could spend a week in Leah's company without telling her how he felt, and he wasn't prepared to embarrass himself.

'Well, I think you should stay in Bindarra Creek, although you might get sick of sleeping in a swag on damp ground. Have you got a groundsheet? There's been a lot of rain lately. The river's higher than I've ever seen it in all the years I lived here.'

'I have.'

'Good.'

'And I'll think about staying. Who knows? We might still be searching for the mistletoe. But I won't promise about the Christmas carols. You know what a Scrooge I am.'

'Well, it's up to me to show you the joy that can be found in Christmas. I'll even see if I can get another pair of elf ears from Josie for you.' Leah's eyes were wide as she looked up at him and it was all Mark could do not to put his arms around her and kiss those gorgeous lips.

'Heaven forbid! Now you've really talked me out of it.' Leah opened the gate before he could succumb to temptation, and he reached up and wiped the perspiration from his brow.

'It is a beautiful home, isn't it?' she said.

'It is.'

'Since all that rain the gardens and lawns are absolutely beautiful. I'd love to have a house like this one day.'

'I hope your dreams come true, Leah. You deserve it.' Mark kept his voice quiet, and he moved back a little so she was out of reach.

'What's your dream, Mark?' Her tone was wistful.

'My dream?' He knew his voice was husky from the emotion he was holding back. 'Honestly, Leah, you wouldn't believe me if I told you.'

'Try me.' In the dim light, he saw her chin go up.

'I'll make you a promise. If we find the mistletoe, I'll tell you my dream.'

'Excellent. We'll have to make sure we find it. You're an enigma, Mark. But a nice one. Now, will you be right to find your way back to the caravan park?'

Mark grinned. 'I'll have to go back to the pub to remember which way I walked before.'

'I forgot you have the most terrible sense of direction. You used to get lost in the museum when you first started.'

'I did, but I've learned my way around now.'

'And how long have you worked there?'

'Almost five years.'

Five years, he thought, since the first day he'd walked into the tea room, and heard this beautiful woman laugh, her green eyes flashing with mirth. Five years since the moment he began to fall for her.

Leah reached for the soft cooler bag. She put it down on the ground and took Mark's arm. The wind caught a strand of her sweet-smelling hair and blew it across his lips.

A jolt of heat ran up to his shoulder at her touch, and he forced himself not to react.

'Now, watch where I'm pointing,' she said. 'Follow this street for two blocks and turn right at the third street—that's Church Street—if you follow it right to the end, you'll see the caravan park on your right when you reach River Road. Don't miss the turn or you'll end up in the cemetery.'

'Dead or lost?' he quipped.

'Ha ha. Mark Altmann does have a sense of humour. That's not the same serious man I've worked with, is it?'

'It is.'

Mark couldn't help himself. He put his hand back on Leah's arm and bent down and briefly brushed his lips across her soft cheek.

'Goodnight, Leah. I'll see you in the

morning.'

Chapter 7

Spending so much of Saturday night at the pub with Mark, and his kiss on her cheek, had fired Leah's imagination, not to mention multiplying the fluttering butterflies in her lower belly. When her alarm went off at seven the next morning, she lay there for a moment trying to leave the dream where Mark had been about to kiss her lips this time. Her cheeks heated as she recalled some of the more sensuous moments in dreams that had lasted all night.

She yawned as she swung her legs over the side of the gorgeous four-poster bed. What a waste, being in a bed like this alone. Her dreams had run rampant all night, and she was in need of a strong coffee to wake her up.

In one of her dreams, they had been out in the bush looking for the mistletoe. Mark had looked up and a sexy smile had tilted his lips as he pointed above their heads. She looked up and a huge bunch of native mistletoe was directly above them.

'You know what that means, Leah?' Mark said.

'It means we've achieved our goal,' she replied. As she watched the mistletoe grew and snaked along the branch, and when she blinked Christmas tinsel was intertwined with the greenery.

'No, it means I have to do what I am supposed to,' he said.

'What you're supposed to?'

'Yes, look now it's turned into a kissing bough.' Mark reached out and held Leah's face gently between his warm hands and looked into her eyes. His lips lingered over hers and she closed her eyes, jumping when the blasted alarm went off.

Tiredness did not go well with frustration; she would have to be very careful to keep her temper even today.

After a quick shower, she made a cup of coffee in the coffee machine that was on an antique tray table in the alcove near the window seat. Crimson velvet drapes matched the soft furnishings on the four-poster bed; it was a very pleasant room. and Leah's tension began to ease as she sat on the edge of the bed and sipped her coffee. Once she'd finished, she rinsed her cup and put it back on the tray before crossing to her suitcase to decide what to wear today. Her usual choice of a summer dress would not be appropriate for a day in the bush. She dug to the bottom and pulled out cargo pants and a short-sleeved T-shirt.

The summer air outside the open window was heavy and humid.

The lace curtains behind the drapes hung still; there was no breeze at all and the forecast temperature was not conducive to trudging around in the bush. With all the recent rain, it would be hot and steamy out there.

Leah couldn't help the grin that crossed her face. Speaking of hot and steamy, she would have to banish all memories of those dreams as she spent the day with Mark.

Excited anticipation filled her. A day to be spent with Mark in a place she loved. Just the two of them, and a *whole* day—not the usual fifteen-minute tea break she had looked forward to every day at the museum.

On her way down to the breakfast room, she detoured via her car and took out her hiking boots. A few times in Sydney, she'd considered throwing them out, but the memories of hiking at Bindarra Creek had ensured she'd held onto them, and she had packed them for this trip along with a thick pair of socks.

I must've known something, she thought.

She ran lightly up the stairs and put the boots beside her backpack; she wouldn't wear them to breakfast. When she went back down, the breakfast room was half-full and she stood at the door looking at the tables.

'Good morning, Leah.' Edwina gestured for her to follow her to a table set for two by the window. 'Come and sit down. Would you like tea or coffee?'

'Coffee would be great, thank you. I must tell you how much I'm enjoying staying at Fig Tree Lodge. The building is beautiful and I love the way you've furnished it.'

'Thank you. We're very happy with it. My grandson, Dodge, owns *The Phoenix* and he's sourced some lovely pieces and restored them for me recently.'

'*The Phoenix*?'

'He and his wife run Tessa's antique shop. It's a couple of doors up from the Cypress Cafe.'

'Oh, I did see that, but I haven't had time to have a browse,' Leah said as she took a seat at the table. She smiled as Edwina flicked open a white linen napkin and placed it on her lap. 'One day, I'll have a home to fill with antiques. That tray table in my room is gorgeous.'

'One day you will, Leah. And that table is one of Dodge's. You should have seen it before he restored it. I thought it was a throwaway. He'll be very pleased to hear that you commented on it. I'll make sure I tell him. He's filling in with the cooking for a couple of days. Lou, my usual cook—

and also my daughter-in-law—has taken her twins to visit her parents for a couple of days.'

'Sounds like Dodge is a man of many talents.'

'He is. Now, would you like a hot breakfast?'

If she was going to be trudging in the bush, Leah knew she needed to make sure she had lots of energy.

'I would, thank you.'

'I'll be back with your coffee in a tick.' Edwina smiled and headed for the kitchen.

Leah checked her messages and email while she waited. She sent a message to Grant Cummings letting him know she wasn't able to call in today but asked if tomorrow would suit him instead.

A reply, *that's fine*, came back immediately.

She texted Mandy, saying how excited she was to be meeting up tonight for dinner and then as Leah put the phone down, Edwina appeared with a coffeepot.

'How are you enjoying being back in Bindarra Creek?' Edwina asked as she placed the pot in the middle of the table.

'Thank you.' Leah smiled up at her. 'I'm enjoying being back in town very much. I'm actually looking at an apartment in Court Street tomorrow.'

'Yes, I heard Grant and Cathy are moving into a rental house on some land while their new house is being built.'

Leah hid a smile. Edwina Lette had always had her finger on the pulse of Bindarra Creek.

'It's been so lovely to see that romance. Cathy deserves happiness in her life and Grant's a lovely man *and* a local. He'll take good care of Cathy and the children.'

'I met them at the Rossiter's on Saturday night. That Josie is full of beans.'

'She's a little tearaway, that one.' Edwina was on for a chat. 'What are your plans for today?'

'It's going to be a rather exciting day,' Leah said. 'One of my colleagues from the museum just happened to be here, and I ran into him. He's working on a project that I was a part of before I left. We're going to the national park looking for a specimen that he's been researching for a while and he's asked me to come along to illustrate it. If we find it.'

'It'll be very hot out there today.' Edwina frowned.

'Yes, I know. I've packed my swimmers.'

'If you do go in the river, be very careful. There are quite a few whirlpools and debris in there at the moment. It's not terribly safe. We've had a few close calls recently.'

'We'll be careful,' Leah said.

'What about some lunch to take with you? I can get Dodge to pack you some sandwiches and some fruit and some water, if you like?'

'Oh, that would be wonderful. Thank you. I'd really appreciate that and do make sure you add it to my bill.'

'Don't worry dear, I will.'

Once she'd finished the scrambled eggs she'd chosen, Leah went back to her room, glancing at the time on her phone as she walked up the stairs. A little anticipatory flutter twirled in her tummy; Mark would be here soon. After brushing her teeth, she put her hair up in a high ponytail to be cool. When her socks and boots were on, she picked up the small backpack that held the essentials for the day.

As Leah made her way downstairs, Edwina came out of the dining room carrying a tray.

'Dodge put your lunch in a cooler bag on the table next to the front door. I've also put a couple of towels there for you in case you do go for a swim.'

'You're making life very easy for me.' Leah chuckled. 'I could get used to this.'

Edwina looked at her intently without speaking for a moment. 'I think that today is going to be good for you, without anything that we do for you here,' she finally said enigmatically.

'I hope so. It would be fabulous if we can find what we're looking for.'

Edwina's eyes were intense. 'I think you'll find what you're looking for, plus much more. Now have a happy day and make the most of it.'

'I will.' Leah collected the food and towels from the antique table in the front hall. As she closed the screen door behind her, Mark pulled up in a shiny green Jeep.

Before he could get out, Leah opened the passenger door, climbed in and turned around, putting her backpack, the cooler bag and the towels on the floor of the back seat.

'Good morning, Mark,' she said trying to forget the explicit dreams she'd had.

'Good morning, Leah.'

She glanced across and noticed the dark shadows under his eyes. 'Did you work late, Mark?'

'I did work late. I got my phone charged and I managed to get onto my laptop I'm a little bit worried though.' He put the Jeep into drive and pulled out onto the road.

'Worried?' she asked with a frown. 'What about?'

'I zoomed in on that photo and I suspect it might not be the plant we're looking for. As you may recall, the image I was sent is a close-up of the flower. I did some comparisons using one of the online plant identification apps.'

'And?' she prompted as he stopped at the stop sign at the end of Willow Drive.

'There is a proliferation of an invasive plant commonly known as Mother-of-millions.'

'Isn't that what they also call Christmas Bells?' Leah asked. She checked to the right as Mark indicated to turn onto Main Street. 'You're clear that way.'

'You're close, but no. The three have a very similar flower, however, *Blandfordia grandiflora*, commonly known as Christmas Bells, is a flowering plant endemic to eastern New South Wales. The flowers are brownish red with yellow tips, not red. Now Mother-of-millions belongs to the genus, *Bryophyllum*, and it's a succulent perennial plant. The flowers are orange-red in colour and occur in a cluster at the top of a single stem.'

'And you think that the photo we thought was the rare mistletoe—'

'Yes, what I was hoping was *Loranthus tetrapetalus*, is possibly the invasive species, a very common species known as Mother-of millions.'

His expression was so woebegone, Leah's heart went out to him.

'So, a wasted trip for you?'

Even if it had been a waste for Mark, Leah would always cherish the day or so they'd had together.

His expression lightened. 'I certainly haven't had a wasted trip. We can still go and look. It will either be successful or it won't.'

'Sounds like a plan.'

'I'll park down here so we can collect some lunch to take with us.'

'No worries. It's all under control. That's what's in the cooler bag I put in the back. Mrs Lette from the lodge has equipped us for a long day. She even gave me towels in case we decide to swim in the river. It's going to be very hot out there today.'

'Yes, we'll notice it when we get out of the air conditioning.'

'We will,' Leah said. 'Now, let's go exploring.'

***

Mark followed Leah's directions as they left town and took the northern road as far as the turn-off to the Akuna National Park. The landscape was lush and green, and the cattle grazing in the paddocks looked healthy and content. Occasionally, he slowed the Jeep as they passed people riding pushbikes, and got cheery waves as they passed.

'Looks like a relaxing Sunday in town,' Leah commented.

Mark nodded, hoping that their day wouldn't be too arduous. He'd dressed in shorts and a T-shirt and put a long sleeve shirt over the top, along with his broad-brimmed straw hat which would protect him from too much sun.

'Did you pack a hat, Leah?'

'Yes, Mum, I did. I've got a hat and I packed suncream, did you?'

Mark's face heated. 'Ah, I have a hat but I didn't think of suncream.'

'Well then, I'll share mine with you, city boy.'

The conversation between them was light and mostly about work as they headed ten kilometres towards the track that Leah had decided would be the best one to follow.

'I do remember a stand of grass trees out on this track. From memory, it goes quite close to the river and there used to be a good swimming hole there but we'll have to be careful if we do swim. Did you think to pack swimmers, Mark?'

He shook his head. 'No, I didn't but I'll be right.'

Leah raised her eyebrows. 'Will you?'

'I will.' He knew his grin was cheeky. He was enjoying the banter with Leah.

At the end of the road where the walking track began, there was a small car park, and as expected at this time of the year, it was empty of cars.

'No one in their right mind would go hiking in this heat,' Leah commented as Mark blinked to clear the perspiration from his eyes. Once he'd turned the engine off, the heat had skyrocketed. 'Although I am sure I did in my teens. The swimming hole at the end of this track was worth the hot walk.'

Mark climbed out first and came around to the passenger side and held open the door for Leah. She smiled at him.

'Thank you,' she said as he held out his hand and helped her out of the high Jeep.

'Pass me your backpack and I'll carry it for you,' he offered.

'I'll get my hat out first,' she said, her eyes twinkling. 'I put my suncream on before you picked me up. Would you like to put some on now?'

'It's okay. I've got a broad-brimmed hat and while we're in the shade of the trees, I'll be fine. If it gets a little bit more open as we walk, I'll put some on then.'

'Suit yourself,' Leah said.

Mark nodded and repeated the instructions that the photographer of the image had given to his contact.

'Four kilometres along the track and then two to three hundred metres to the east, and then we need to look out for a stand of grass trees.' He focused on the track ahead, occasionally checking the app on this watch to see how far they'd walked.

The track was high and the recent rains had drained away any rainwater; it was only when they went down the occasional decline that they had to take care where they walked in the slippery mud.

Mark pointed to a particularly disturbed patch of wet earth. 'What sort of animal tracks are they?'

Leah walked over and examined the mud. 'I think you'll find there are wombats around here.'

'I'll look out for them,' Mark said. He touched Leah's shoulder and then pointed as excitement filled him. She stepped back beside him and he could feel the warmth of her back against his chest. 'Look, there's an echidna.'

They stood close and watched the black spiky monotreme before it lumbered awkwardly across the track and disappeared into the long grass. Mark's focus quickly moved from the echidna; he let his gaze rake over the elegant lines of Leah's neck.

Mark knew he couldn't continue like this. He was going to have to tell her what he was feeling. The thought of leaving her and going back to the museum and never seeing her again unsettled him. But did he have the courage to do it?

What could happen if he declared his

feelings?

She could laugh.

No, she was too kind for that.

But she could be embarrassed and decide not to spend any more time with him.

His mind churned as they walked along. He was damned if he did, and damned if he didn't.

Mark nodded to himself as he came to a decision. He would ask Leah out to dinner tonight. He would make it a real date.

They turned as one and kept walking, both keeping their eyes focused on each side of the track.

Occasionally, a parrot would squawk and fly away as they walked through its habitat.

'I'm pleased to see you had your hiking boots with you.' Mark finally broke the silence. 'Keep an eye out for snakes.'

'There's a lot of water around. We will have to be careful,' Leah said with a shiver.

Mark checked his watch after twenty minutes of walking. 'We've come about two and a half kilometres. Would you like to have a break for a while?'

'I'm fine, but we should stop and have a drink to keep hydrated,' Leah said.

'Good plan.'

They stopped in the shade of a huge old gum tree and Mark opened the backpack and took out two bottles of water, opened one and passed it to Leah.

As she lifted the bottle to her lips, she tilted her head back and it brought to mind one of the more explicit dreams he'd had about her last night.

Spending so much time with Leah had kicked his imagination into overdrive and she'd been in his dreams all night.

When she screwed the top back on the bottle her lips were moist and pink, and Mark closed his eyes so he wasn't looking at her damp lips.

'What's wrong?' she asked. 'You're not overheated, are you?'

Not from the heat of the day, Mark thought.

'I'm fine,' he said. 'Let's go.' His tone may have been a bit terse, but it was because he knew he was kidding himself. There was no way Leah Maclean was a bit interested in him.

As they walked the next kilometre Mark imagined working at the museum with no Leah there. Half the joy of his work had been sharing his working life with her, knowing she was in the same place. He should have asked her out a long time ago.

At least he knew where she'd be; he could imagine her living in this town and being quite happy. He knew she'd make a success of her new career. She had the personality and communication skills that would help her make contacts and find plenty of work. And her talent was amazing.

Even though it would be hard not to have her at the museum, Mark genuinely hoped that she would make a success of her new career.

'Penny for your thoughts,' she said, stepping back to walk beside him as the track widened. The sound of flowing water began to reach them from ahead.

This is your chance, he told himself. *Don't stuff up.*

'Funny, you should ask that. I was just thinking about you living out here and hoping that your new career goes well for you.'

'I haven't really quite decided yet that I will stay.'

Hope flared.

'But you have left the museum?'

'Yes, I'm determined to follow through with my plan to become an illustrator. I just don't know where I'll base myself yet.'

'I'm sure you'll do well, wherever you decide to work from. You have the personality to do it.'

'Thank you. I hope you're right. I'd like to focus on children's books, but I guess I'll have to go with whatever pays as I start off. I could do some scientific illustrations for the university and I know

I can get work. What I have to decide is whether I am going to move out here or whether I'll go back to my apartment in the city.'

'So, you haven't given up your apartment yet?' That spark of hope grew a little more.

'No, I wanted to come out and see if Bindarra Creek was what I remembered.'

'And it is?'

'It's even better than I remembered. Everyone is so friendly and I think it would be a very easy community to settle into.'

'Where would you live, if you could live anywhere you chose?'

'If I could live anywhere?' Leah tipped her head to the side and closed her eyes. Her voice was dreamy. 'I'd live in an old sandstone homestead on a couple of acres, filled with antiques and surrounded by grapevines. It would have magnificent old gardens and a studio that looked out to the mountains or over the river.'

He was quiet for a moment. 'I'll miss you, Leah.'

Her head flew up and their eyes connected briefly before he looked down at his watch.

'We've covered the distance now. We need to keep an eye out for that stand of grass trees that you thought was along this track.'

Leah nodded and put her hand to her eyes

looking to the east.

Chapter 8

Leah tried to stop her hand from shaking as she shaded her eyes

and stared into the bush. Mark said he was going to *miss* her.

Was he going to miss *her*, or was he going to miss working with her?

There were two very different types of missing. A slight breeze drifted across and Leah narrowed her eyes as waving green grass fronds against the clear blue sky caught her eye.

'There,' she said. 'Over there. I can just see the tops of the grass trees as they swayed in that bit of breeze.'

'Excellent.' Mark held out his hand. 'Take my hand. We'll stay close as we walk through that long grass. If we make enough noise, hopefully we'll scare away any snakes that might be lurking in there.'

Leah took the smooth, warm hand that he offered, and ignored the heat that ran up her arm as his fingers closed around hers. Mark held her hand firmly as he stepped into the long grass at the side of the track.

Leah was so focused on the feel of his skin against hers, she barely heard the rustling of the grass as they walked through the bush to the stand of grass trees.

'Oh no.' Mark came to an abrupt stop and she almost collided with him. He turned and his other hand took her elbow and held her steady.

'What is it? A snake?' she said, widening her eyes. She might have grown up out here in the bush, but she was still very wary of snakes.

'No. Look.' His voice held disappointment as he let go of her, and dropped his hand.

Mark stepped to the side, and Leah looked ahead.

In front of them was a clearing surrounded by tall eucalypts. Leaf litter covered the clearing in front of them, the brown of dead leaves contrasting with the colourful sight that had disappointed Mark so much. Dozens and dozens of orange-red flowers clustered at the top of single stems covered the large clear area ahead.

'*Bryophyllum*,' he said despondently.

Leah couldn't help herself. She reached out and took his hand and squeezed. 'I'm sorry, Mark. The photographer was obviously confused.'

'He must have been. I should have looked more closely before I left Sydney,' he said.

'I remember this plant now. It's toxic to

cattle, isn't it?'

'Not only to cattle,' Mark replied. 'Mother-of-millions is toxic when ingested by livestock; it is also poisonous to humans and pets. There's enough in front of us to kill a herd of cattle.'

'There wouldn't be any cattle in the national park though, would there?' she asked with a frown.

'I didn't see any, but we'll have to report this outbreak, just in case,' Mark said.

'I'm sorry, Mark. I know how excited you were.'

'It's okay. Part of the job,' he said, but she could hear the disappointment in his voice. 'Come on, we'll head back before it gets hotter.'

'Let's walk down to the river. It's a waste to come this far and not show you. The Akuna River is really pretty.'

'If you'd like to.'

'I would. Come on, cheer up, it's not the end of the world. You have the adventure of still looking ahead.'

This time as they walked back to the track, Mark didn't hold her hand. Leah supposed he thought any snakes that may have been lingering would be long gone with them clumping through the bush.

'The river's only a hundred or so metres down the track.' She caught up to him. 'I'm hot enough for a swim. What do you think?'

His face brightened as he looked at her. 'You're good for the soul, Leah. A swim would be good, as long as you don't mind me going in my jocks.'

Chapter 9

Mark held his breath as he sat on the towel Leah had spread on the grassy river bank. As she'd said, it was a very pretty spot. The water was clear enough to see the stones in the shallow reaches of the pool in front of them, and small brown fish darted in and out of the shadows. Two weeping willows draped gracefully into the water, and small birds swooped and dipped into the slow-flowing river. The branches of a solid gum tree reached out over the pool, and someone had tied a rope swing onto the lowest branch.

But it wasn't the beauty of the scene that had made Mark catch and hold his breath. Leah had stepped behind the willows to get changed into her swimmers. He heard the rustle of leaves and he turned just as she walked out through the lacy fronds.

Oh my God. His mouth dried and blood thrummed through his body.

She looked like a Greek goddess. A white one-piece swimming costume moulded her slim figure, plunging to a vertical row of small, gold buttons that went from between her breasts to her waist, giving a tantalising glimpse of olive skin.

Her legs were long and lithe, and Mark's body reacted instantly to her beauty.

'Are you going to come in with me?' Leah called as she went to the edge of the bank. 'It's quite safe, the bend upriver has created quite a calm pool here.' She leaned forward and trailed her fingers in the water. 'It's lovely and cool. Come on, don't be a squib.'

'I'll be there in a minute,' Mark managed to choke out. He'd have to wait until her back was turned before he could shed his shorts and jump into the water, or it was going to be embarrassing for both of them.

He needed a good dash of cold water.

Leah slid into the water and as she swam across the pool, he quickly jumped up, stripped down to his jocks, raced over to the water and jumped in near where the rope swung over the river.

'Holy hell,' he yelled. 'It's not cool, it's freezing!' His grin was wide though; the icy cold water had certainly done the trick.

Mark dived beneath the water and opened his eyes fascinated by the flora that was swaying in the water. He swam along the bottom until he couldn't hold his breath any longer and pushed up to the surface.

As his head broke through the water, his

legs brushed something solid, and he jumped.

He blinked the water from his eyes and stared into Leah's face.

'Sorry, I didn't realise you were over here.'

'No problem. It's lovely, isn't it?'

'Yes,' he said softly as he stared at her. Long eyelashes held little droplets of water, and her cheeks held a pink tinge from the exertion of her swim in the cold water. 'Very lovely.'

Mark tipped his head back, and a bolt of disbelief hit him.

He widened his eyes and his mouth opened.

Leah's hand came to his shoulder and her voice held worry. 'What is it? Do you have a cramp from the cold water?'

He shook his head and kept staring at the tree above.

Leah's other hand rested on his shoulder, and it was a natural movement for his hands to drop to her waist and hold her.

'Look up above us, Leah.'

She tipped her head back and he watched as realisation dawned. Her lips opened in a perfect O, and her eyes widened. 'Oh my gosh! Is it? Is it what I think it is?'

'It is.' His voice was husky, as he held himself back. He could feel her trembling beneath his hands. He took a breath to steady himself.

'*Loranthus tetrapetalus*' she whispered.

'Our elusive native mistletoe.'

Leah lowered her head and their eyes met. His heart pounded as she spoke.

'And we're under the mistletoe. Do you know the tradition, Mark?'

'I do.'

Leah lifted her hands from his shoulders and touched his cheeks as he held her steady in the water. Her lips were slightly parted as he drowned in her eyes.

So tempting. So very, very tempting.

He lowered his head and took her lips with his.

So, so sweet.

Leah's lips were warm beneath his, and all his hesitation fled as she responded. Mark deepened the kiss and her mouth opened to him.

Their first kiss was perfection.

'And in a perfect place,' Leah said. Mark hadn't realised he had spoken aloud.

He lifted her into his arms and walked across the smooth stones in the shallow water. Stepping up the low bank, Mark crossed to the blue and white striped towel and kneeled with her in his arms before laying her down gently.

'I've dreamed about this for so long,' he said.

Her mouth tilted in a smile as he looked down at her. 'As I have.'

Mark shook his head. 'We've wasted so much time.'

'No, it was meant to be,' Leah said. 'The perfect time and the perfect place.'

Mark lay beside her and took the woman he loved into his arms.

With small birds flitting around them, and the branches sighing above them, he lowered his mouth to hers again. The feel of her cool, damp hands on his back was heaven as Leah caressed his skin.

Time drifted along with the sound of the water burbling beside them. Each time he lifted his head, Leah's lips were curved in a soft smile.

'Perfection,' he murmured.

Epilogue

Edwina Lette had been more than happy to have Mark join Leah in her room at Fig Tree Lodge. Each morning when they went down to breakfast, she smiled at them, and Leah knew that her smile held secrets.

Edwina had known what the day at the river would bring; the happiness it had brought to both of them.

Leah couldn't believe that Mark had resigned from the museum. He'd sent an email to Herman this afternoon.

'If you're moving to Bindarra Creek, would it bother you, if I moved here too?' he asked as they walked home from the showgrounds where the Christmas carols had been held.

Ah, so that was what was wrong with him tonight.

Mark had seemed nervy all night. He'd been attentive, but she'd sensed there was something worrying him. Leah had wondered if it was because she'd taken him to the Christmas carols, but he'd assured her that he was enjoying the festivities in town.

'I'd be moving back to Sydney if you were there,' she said squeezing his fingers.

'This is a much nicer place to live. I can work remotely too.'

'We've waited long enough, Mark.' Leah smiled. 'It's a wonderful community. Did you see the look on Josie's face when she spotted your arm around me?'

'I did. And I loved her enthusiasm when she played her triangle in the school band.'

'She certainly put everything into it. And what about that guy who sang *O Holy Night?* His voice gave me goosebumps.'

Mark nodded. 'He was amazing. Ryan said that was Mrs Lette's son-in-law.'

'I didn't know that. I love the connections in this town,' Leah said with a smile. Her smile was all the wider because she'd seen how much Mark had enjoyed the carols.

'And I like all of your friends I've met so far. There's just one thing that might upset the apple cart though.'

Leah paused. 'What? What's wrong?'

'Do you think Grant would be upset if you didn't move into his duplex?'

'Why? Where else would we live?'

Mark smiled as she said "we" and he leaned over and kissed her. It was a while before the conversation resumed.

'When you were having coffee with Mandy

yesterday, I did some shopping. Edwina took me to her grandson's antique store and I also went to see the local real estate agent, Hunter Sullivan.'

'Has another rental come up?' Leah asked. 'There was nothing else available last week.'

'No,' Mark said. 'But I've bought you a Christmas present.'

'A Christmas present?'

'I might be rushing you so if you want to slow me down, Grant's apartment is still available.'

'You're talking in circles, Mark.'

Mark opened the gate to Fig Tree Lodge and led Leah over to sit on the wrought iron seat under the branches of the large spreading tree in the front garden. Leah stared as he got down on one knee in front of her. She put her hand to her mouth.

'This might be too soon, but I can't give you your big present until I check that you will accept this one.'

'My big present?' Leah frowned as his voice shook.

Mark reached into his pocket and took out a small velvet box. Leah drew in a sharp breath as he flicked it open.

'I hope you don't mind that it's not new, but when I saw it, I knew it was perfect for you.'

A square amethyst in a silver filigree setting winked at her in the soft moonlight. 'Will you marry me, Leah?'

Tears filled her eyes as she reached down and took his face in her hands. 'I will, Mark.'

He slipped the ring onto her finger, and it was a perfect fit.

'Edwina knew what I was thinking; she's a mind reader, that woman. She took me to meet Dodge. As soon as I saw this, I knew it was meant for you.'

'It's beautiful, Mark.'

He rose and sat beside her and took her into his arms. 'We'll seal our engagement with a kiss, and then I'll tell you about your other present.'

'You are enough of a Christmas present for me,' Leah murmured against his mouth.

All was quiet for a long while.

Finally, Mark lifted his head and rested his cheek against hers. 'Tomorrow, I'll take you for a drive.'

'A drive?' she murmured. Leah's limbs were light and fluid, as happiness reached every inch of her body.

'You know how you said you'd love an old house like this, filled with antiques and surrounded by a lovely garden and grapevines?'

'Did I?'

'You did.'

'So, a drive?'

'Yes. Last week one of the old vineyards on Mt Ingalls Road came on the market, but it's not available anymore.'

'But you thought I'd like to see the house?'

'I thought you'd like to see *our* new house.' Mark's smile was wide as she looked into the face of the man she loved.

'Oh, Mark, are you serious? You couldn't have. You shouldn't have. They cost millions out there.'

'I did. Let's say I made Hunter Sullivan a very happy real estate agent. And it doesn't matter what it cost. My grandparents left me a very wealthy man. I know that my grandmother would have loved you, and she'd be delighted to see where we're going to live and raise our children.'

Tears were rolling down Leah's face, and she sniffed as Mark lifted his hand and wiped them away. 'How can I ever find a present for you to equal this?' she said her voice trembling.

'You've already given me the best present you ever could,' Mark said as his arms went around her again. 'Your love.'

A soft breeze moved the leaves above and the stars beamed down on them as they pledged their love to each other.

Edwina Lette smiled as she quietly closed the gate behind her, but the lovers were not even aware of her walking past. She had known that Leah and Mark would make their home together in Bindarra Creek.

THE END

Thank you for reading my Bindarra Creek Christmas Romance, *A Clever Christmas*.

Welcome to the heart-warming joy of nine sweet, Christmas romances set in a small rural town. Experience happy-ever-afters along with the uplifting good cheer of love and life in Bindarra Creek, and meet again our community of interesting and charming people. Each story can be read as a stand-alone and can be read in any order.

The Mistletoe Wish by Suzanne Gilchrist
A Clever Christmas by Annie Seaton
Mistletoe Magic by Erin Moira O'Hara
Christmas Jinx by Susanne Bellamy
Tangled by Tinsel by Phillipa Nefri Clark
The Grinch of Bindarra Creek by Lindsay Douglas
Mistletoe and Blue Jeans by Linda Charles
Christmas at Forrest Glen by Rhonda Forrest
A Cowboy for Christmas by Lauren K McKellar

Buy links:
https://bindarracreekromance.com/bindarra-creek-christmas-romances/

Our Bindarra Creek Christmas Romances are the fifth series set in our fictional small town.

The fourth, is the Bindarra Creek Mystery Romances – a series of seven exciting and suspense-filled romances which again can be read alone.

Buy links can be found here:
https://bindarracreekromance.com/a-bindarra-creek-mystery/

Or on Amazon:
https://www.amazon.com/A-Bindarra-Creek-Mystery-7-book-series/dp/B09V7ZQ9BG

Thank you for reading *A Clever Christmas*.

Below you will find an extract from another Christmas story from me:

You can find *Christmas with the Boss* <u>here</u>.

It's a favourite as it is set at my local beach, and with a true ghost story.

Chapter One
Christmas Eve

Jilly Henderson joined the end of the queue at the only gas station in the quiet little beachside town of Sandy Heads. She folded her arms and settled in for a long wait; it was Christmas Eve and it appeared everyone was stocking up on their last-minute snacks before the shops shut for Christmas Day. Glancing down, she smiled as a pair of large, tanned, sandy, *and* bare feet in front caught her attention. She straightened and lifted her eyes a fraction, enjoying the sight of tightly-muscled calves above those bare feet. Tilting her chin higher, her leisurely perusal continued up tanned skin lightly brushed with blond hair, up to firm thighs that disappeared into a pair of board shorts molding one of the most perfect male butts she had ever seen. Down south, her feminine bits that had been dormant for *way* too long gave a little jiggle.

"Always check out the size of their feet, girls.

Big feet, big—"

"Sharyn!" The giggles that had gone around the office contrasted with the corporate black suits and classy chignons of the executive assistants on the tenth floor of the bank building in George Street. Between the bouts of frantic activity that happened on the trading floor twenty-four hours a day, Jilly spent most of her work day shaking her head at Shaz's antics and hilarious advice.

Blonde-haired and elegant Shaz always managed to come up with a dry comment to break the tense atmosphere of the trading floor. The one about checking out the size of a guy's feet before accepting a date had the girls howling with laughter.

'Because you know what that means, ladies!'

When the boss had lifted his head and frowned through the glass wall of his office, they all quickly put their heads down and focused on the colored numbers on their screens.

Now Jilly stared down at the feet of the guy in front of her. Not that he'd be interested in her, but this guy had *big* feet.

Huge feet. Sharyn would say that was a yes. Jilly stifled a grin and let out a soft sigh; the pretty young things chattering away in front of him were keeping his attention on the front of the queue. Surfer boy wouldn't be interested in a tired and frazzled city girl.

She hadn't been on a date for over a year, so she hadn't had a chance to put Sharyn's test into practice. *And* those girly quivers below were few and far between these days, so that little tremble low in her belly did put a smile on her face. Memories were nice.

Jilly needed no one; she was here at the beach to have a total break. Work had been hectic leading up to the festive season, and with many nights of Christmas functions, drinks and farewells she was feeling burned out.

Five days of bliss, alone, no work and no one to bother her beckoned.

Mr. Big Feet took a step forward as the queue moved and Jilly shuffled along closer to the counter. Her gaze lingered on that tight butt, clad in snug-fitting boardshorts, before she lifted her eyes to feast on a golden tanned back. No harm in looking.

Oh, my. She swallowed.

Broad shoulders lightly dappled with freckles had a sprinkling of sand stuck to the smooth skin. Small grains were embedded in the sexy hollow at the top of his shoulder. It made her think of lazy afternoons lying on the sand. Jilly literally had to curl her fingers to stop herself from reaching up and brushing the sand away. Maybe the surf god wouldn't be impressed if a tired and stressed-looking woman with dark circles beneath her eyes ran her fingers over that glorious back. To distract herself, she turned away and looked out at the cars in the fuel bay, trying to pick which one was his.

Of course. A beat up 1970s Kombi van with two surfboards secured to the roof racks was at the front of the line. Jilly nodded to herself; that would be surfer boy's car. How good would it be to jump in with him and head up the coast to Byron Bay? That was sure to be his destination—a mecca for surf gods.

A girl could dream.

Another step forward in the queue and she turned her gaze back to him, unable to resist one last look.

His curly brown hair was sun-bleached on top, and the thick, springy curls just brushed his shoulders. Even his neck was strong and tanned.

She fanned herself as her wicked imagination kicked into overdrive and tilted her face up toward the frigid air blowing from the vents in the high ceiling. Even though artificial, the air was blessedly cool. A welcome relief after the strong smell of petrol that had pervaded the hot bay as she'd filled her car. It was just on dark, but Jilly was sure the mercury was still registering over thirty degrees outside.

Summer down under. *Bliss.*

Not to mention her internal temperature was sizzling as the erotic fantasy filled her mind. What a sad life she must lead to be fantasizing in a gas station! This short holiday was *way* overdue.

It had been a long, long drive from Sydney. The sooner she found the beach cottage and fell into bed the better. Exhaling with a tired sigh, Jilly shuffled forward another step as the queue moved at a snail pace.

"No, the party's at the surf club *tonight*."

Jilly tilted her head to the side, looking past the surf god's broad shoulders towards the girl who was chatting to the cashier. Mary, the cashier—Jilly could just see her name tag—reached for the milk that the customer had placed on the counter. The register beeped as she scanned the plastic container.

"Tonight? I thought the party at the surf club was on New Year's Eve?" The pretty young girl in a red sarong pushed her hair back from her face as she lifted the rest of her groceries onto the counter. Her voice rose shrilly.

Mary chewed gum as she shook her head—no rush here. The dozen or so customers in the queue ahead of Jilly almost let out a collective sigh as they jiggled their feet, tapped hands on thighs and looked at their watches. Even the surf god's shoulders tensed a little, sending another pleasant little ripple through her belly.

Country service.

But Jilly liked it; people-watching was fun, even if she was tired. In Sydney, you were lucky to get a hello in any store. Now Mary, the slow-moving cashier, leaned on one elbow and imparted the correct information about this party to anyone who was interested. "No, it's tonight. Starts in a couple of hours."

"Really?" The girl in the red sarong leaned forward. "Are you sure?"

"Yes, it's at the surf club *tonight*. The New Year's Eve *party* is at the pub on the river."

"Well, I'm not missing either of them. Have you seen the talent in town this week?" Jilly resisted a nod as the 'talent' in front of her stretched to his toes and the muscles in his calves flexed.

"All the local surfers are home for Christmas and the parties will be hot!" The young girl pushed her hair back from her face as she turned apologetically to the person in the queue behind her. "Sorry, I remembered I just have to grab some party supplies. Won't take a minute." She flicked a glance back to the cashier and her mouth split into a grin. "Just as well I've already been to the bottle shop."

"Got your priorities right there, love." Mary, the cashier's, voice held a tinge of sarcasm.

"Oh, for God's sake." Impatience filled Jilly as she watched the girl head for the fridges lining the back wall. The next customer in line stepped up to the other register but Mary waved him away.

"Sorry, love. The other cashier is on a tea break. You'll have to wait." She flicked open a magazine on the counter and began to read, ignoring the cross mutterings of the waiting customers.

Jilly closed her mouth as another yawn threatened.

What was one more delay? Her day had been fraught with them since she'd hit that first red traffic light in Manly this morning. Anyone would think she was having a bad luck day. Black cats, ladders, broken mirrors, shoes on tables—her dad had been a sucker for superstitions and Jilly knew them all. She swallowed as she pushed that thought away; her grief was on hold until she was ready to deal with it.

The entire trip up the coast from Sydney had been a nightmare from start to finish. Heavy traffic had choked the M1 as what had seemed like the entire population of the city, headed for the beaches of the north for the annual break between Christmas Eve and the New Year. Dad had always told her not to leave Sydney on Christmas Eve, but Jilly had been so keen to get away from the city after the funeral, she'd decided to put up with the traffic.

But it had turned into a ten-hour trip, instead of

the five it should have taken. Despite the six-lane freeway, a broken-down truck near the Gosford interchange had added two hours to her trip. Finally, after crawling through slow bumper-to-bumper traffic, she'd called into a small town just south of her destination to stock up on groceries for her eight-day break. Once she got to the beach cottage, she had no intention of getting back in her car until she left after the New Year.

Keen to travel the last short leg of the trip, she'd hurried out to her small sedan with her few grocery bags and groaned. An old, battered utility had her car parked in. Jilly had sat on the grass verge in the hot sun, fuming for half an hour until an elderly couple pushed their laden trolley across the car park. The words that she'd had ready to blast the car's owner died away as she watched the old man hold his wife's hand and place her carefully in the front seat, before he slowly unpacked the trolley into the back of the ute. Jilly couldn't help herself. She pushed to her feet and helped him unload.

"Thank you, my dear." He went around to the front of the car and came back with a small parcel and pressed it into her hands. "Merry Christmas. One of Ethel's plum puddings for you."

Tears welled into Jilly's eyes and she ran the back of her hand over her face; emotion had clogged her throat for the whole trip, but she wasn't going to give in. "Merry Christmas to you and your wife too."

He drove away sedately; still oblivious that he had blocked in Jilly's car. With a sigh, she'd pulled out and hit the highway again.

Smothering a yawn with the back of her hand, she rocked on her feet as she waited and looked over to the brightly-coloured products on the shelves along the wall. Everything to tempt the sweet tooth she tried her best not to indulge.

Bad move. On the back seat of her car were three bags filled with salad makings, and fruit. Shaz and Elise, the perpetual dieters at work had taught her good habits; there was no Christmas cheer for her apart from Ethel's plum pudding. Jilly smiled as she stepped away from the queue. She was at the rear, so if she was quick, she wouldn't lose her place.

Picking up a basket she headed to the fridge and opened the door. A minute later her basket was filled with a carton of custard to go with the plum pudding, five small bottles of full-cream strawberry-flavoured milk—she wouldn't tell the girls at work—two family-size chocolate bars and two trashy magazines. Jilly stepped between the shelves and threw in two bags of potato chips for good measure on her way back to the queue. No one had joined it and she got to stand behind the surf god again.

The girl in the sarong was still loading her basket. It was Christmas; Jilly had to dig deep to find some Christmas spirit. Finally, the girl came back to the counter, paid for her party goodies and the queue began to move more quickly. There were now only seven customers ahead of Jilly and she covered another yawn with one hand.

A second cashier appeared behind the counter and the queue moved again. Jilly reached down to pick up her basket as surfer boy reached the head of the queue and paid for his fuel. Bending down, she reached for her basket as he turned to pass her. She glanced his way as she straightened. Did the face match the perfect body?

Oh. My. God.

Jilly froze and forced her open mouth to close. If you *could* freeze when prickles of heat scorched your skin.

"Miss Henderson." Her boss, the senior group executive and chair of the Executive Committee of the SBA bank stopped walking and flashed a smile at her. Perfect white teeth, the same sexy grin that she'd admired every day for the past six months. She'd tried to ignore her good-looking boss since he'd arrived at the bank mid-year. But now, the tailored business suit had been replaced with a bare chest and those low-slung boardshorts, and the fantasy of the last ten minutes now left her gasping for composure. Her mouth dried as she stared at the V of dark blond hair that disappeared into the shorts below his navel. The muscles on his chest were as ripped as the rest of him. Who could ever have known what that business suit hid?

"Mr Smythe-Phillips," she finally managed to croak out.

"Feeling peckish, are you, Miss Henderson?"

"What?" Jilly lifted her eyes from his bare stomach to meet a pair of eyes crinkled with laughter.

Sprung perving at his chest. How embarrassing.

His grin widened as he pointed to her plastic basket.

Relief flooded through her; he was talking about the food. Jilly swallowed and forced the huskiness from her voice. "Ah yes, um . . . er . . . um . . . some holiday supplies," she stuttered and stumbled over her words like a teenage girl with a crush.

Thank God, he hadn't noticed her when she'd been salivating over him in the queue. There was no way she could have sustained a conversation with him for any length of time with him half-naked in front of her; she would have died of embarrassment. It was bad enough to be caught out in a pair of skimpy shorts, and a tight-fitting T-shirt. At least he was on his way out and she didn't have to make social conversation for long.

"See you back at the office next week. Have a good Christmas . . .Jilly." His voice was as deep and sexy as ever and her name rolled off his tongue. She'd never noticed what a sexy voice he had before.

Jilly nodded mutely.

He really was just too gorgeous; for six months she'd managed to hide how she'd dreamed about Dominic Smythe-Phillips. And that was when he was in a business suit. Now he'd morphed into a tanned surfing god, she was a goner. How the hell she'd ever sit across the board table without thinking of that bare chest when she went back to work . . .

Jilly stared after Dominic as he opened the door of the silver Audi TT Roadster that was parked behind the Kombi van. Wrong again.

Little warm tingles were having a fun time down in the now ex-dormant zone.

"Stop perving and hurry up, love. You're holding up the queue." Mary's drawl was amused as her gaze followed Jilly's. "Bit of a looker, is our Dom, isn't he?"

Jilly closed her mouth and turned to the waiting cashier.

A BINDARRA CREEK DUO

Our Dom?

Chapter Two

Dominic Henderson turned his sleek sports sedan onto the dirt road that skirted the beach. He deliberately looked away from the first cottage and turned his attention towards the beach. Purple shadows cast by the setting sun hovered on the glassy water. The last rays caught the slow-moving swell as it pushed to shore, breaking as a bridal veil of foam on the wet sand. Even though the waves were small, there was a nice right-hand break on the point, just catching the last glimmers of light from the sun as it sank below the Great Dividing Range to the west of Sandy Heads, the small town where he'd learned to surf.

Should be great for a surf in the morning.

But surfing tomorrow wasn't at the forefront of his thoughts. The skimpy shorts and the figure-hugging tank top were very different to the attire of Miss Henderson of the corporate suits and high heels. If it hadn't been for the glorious copper-toned hair that cascaded down her back, Dominic probably wouldn't even have recognized the woman behind him as his executive assistant. The lush image imprinted on his mind since Jilly Henderson had gaped up at him in the gas station wouldn't go away. The same woman who had caught his eye the day he had been appointed as chief of the Group Executive at the biggest bank in Sydney. There'd been muttered comments about special treatment when she'd been promoted to his executive assistant, but it hadn't taken much to dispel the gossip. He was used to it; corporate banking was a bitchy and cutthroat environment. He recognized talent and hard work; good looks were a bonus.

He wondered idly where she was heading and then focused on the surf. They hadn't shared their Christmas plans; the office was too busy for personal conversations. And he much preferred to keep work businesslike without the social chitchat that went on in the lunchroom.

Kept the rumours at bay. Although he did wonder what Jilly Henderson had been up to lately. Usually one to stay late at her desk, in the last month she'd been leaving as soon as trading ceased for the day, and then she'd had a few days off last week. Personal time, she'd said with no further explanation. She got her work done, so it was none of his business.

Dominic shrugged as he turned to the ocean. And she did her work very well; she had a keen eye for the stock market and on more than one occasion Jilly Henderson had directed his attention to recent trends before he'd noticed them.

Forget work. He was here for a break.

If the swell stayed small, he'd get his knee board out and wax it ready for the morning. Didn't matter that it would be Christmas Day; he had no family left in town.

Nice legs, though.

It had probably been stupid to come up here in his rare time off from work, but it was as good a time as any to try to put his memories to rest. Long overdue.

And cute freckles too.

He'd hit the sack as soon as he'd waxed his board. Pleasant tiredness tugged at Dominic's muscles; he'd been in the water all day on his large board. He'd hit the surf early again tomorrow; his knee board should still be in the small wooden shed attached to the old building at the back of the cottage.

The familiar and long-loved smell of salt and seaweed met Dominic as he climbed out of the Audi. He grabbed the carton of beer he'd picked up from the pub and walked through the long grass to the old cottage. He'd have to pull out Pa's old mower while he was staying here. He stood on the front steps and looked back down the road. It had been a long time since he and Derro had walked together down that road on their way to high school . . . and to the surf. When they'd been teenagers without a worry in the world.

And it had been almost as long since he'd last been down to the other cottage: his grandparents' cottage. Not since Derro's funeral. Dominic pushed open the door and the fresh smell of the ocean was replaced by the musty smell of an old house that had been locked up for a long time.

Pretty eyes too.

He grinned again as green cat-like eyes fixed on his stomach flashed into his head. The prim Miss Henderson had been checking him out. He'd never noticed those cute freckles on her nose either. Maybe he'd break his own rule and ask Jilly Henderson out for dinner when they got back to the city.

Other Books by the Author

OTHER BOOKS from ANNIE

Whitsunday Dawn
Undara
Osprey Reef
East of Alice

Porter Sisters Series

Kakadu Sunset
Daintree
Diamond Sky
Hidden Valley
Larapinta
Kakadu Dawn

Pentecost Island Series
Pippa
Eliza
Nell
Tamsin
Evie
Cherry
Odessa
Sienna

A BINDARRA CREEK DUO

Tess
Isla

The Augathella Girls Series
Outback Roads
Outback Sky
Outback Escape
Outback Wind
Outback Dawn
Outback Moonlight
Outback Dust
Outback Hope
An Augathella Surprise
An Augathella Baby
An Augathella Spring

Sunshine Coast Series
Waiting for Ana
The Trouble with Jack
Healing His Heart
Sunshine Coast Boxed Set

The Richards Brothers Series
The Trouble with Paradise
Marry in Haste
Outback Sunrise
Richards Brothers Boxed Set

Bondi Beach Love Series

ANNIE SEATON

Beach House
Beach Music
Beach Walk
Beach Dreams
The House on the Hill

Second Chance Bay Series
Her Outback Playboy
Her Outback Protector
Her Outback Haven
Her Outback Paradise
The McDougalls of Second Chance Bay Boxed Set

Love Across Time Series
Come Back to Me
Follow Me
Finding Home
The Threads that Bind
Love Across Time 1-4 Boxed Set

Bindarra Creek
Worth the Wait
Full Circle
Secrets of River Cottage
A Clever Christmas
A Place to Belong

A BINDARRA CREEK DUO

Four Seasons Short and Sweet
Ten Days in Paradise
Follow the Sun

Others
Deadly Secrets
Adventures in Time
Silver Valley Witch
The Emerald Necklace
Christmas with the Boss
Her Christmas Star
One Summer in Tuscany

About the Author

Annie lives in Australia, on the beautiful north coast of New South Wales. She sits in her writing chair and looks out over the tranquil Pacific Ocean.

She writes contemporary romance and loves telling stories that always have a happily ever after. She lives with her very own hero of many years and they share their home with Toby, the naughtiest dog in the universe, and Barney, the ragdoll puss, who hides when the four grandchildren come to visit.

Stay up to date with her latest releases at her website: http://www.annieseaton.net

2023: Winner of the long contemporary RUBY award for Larapinta

Finalist for the NZ KORU award 2018 and 2020.

Winner ...Best Established Author of the Year 2017 AUSROM

Long listed for the Sisters in Crime Davitt Awards 2016, 2017, 2018, 2019

Finalist in Book of the Year, Long Romance, RWA Ruby Awards 2016 Kakadu Sunset

Winner ...Best Established Author of the Year 2015 AUSROM

Winner ...Author of the Year 2014 AUSROM

Best Established Author, Ausrom Readers' Choice 2017

Book of the Year (Whitsunday Dawn) Ausrom Readers' Choice Awards 2018

Acknowledgements

As always, a special thank you to my fabulous editors, Susanne Bellamy and Rhonda Forrest, my eagle-eyed proof-readers, Roby Aiken, Anna Welch, and Kristen Woolgar.

A special thank you to Suzanne Gilchrist for coming up with the concept of the Bindarra Creek series.

A Bindarra Creek Duo

Full Circle
Copyright © 2019, Annie Seaton

A Clever Christmas
Copyright © 2022, Annie Seaton